"Feeling rough?" a sympathetic male voice asked, close to her ear.

Her eyes flew open. As her vision adjusted, a lean, attractive face, the jaw rough with morning stubble, came into focus.

He was lying beside her, propped on one elbow, a sheet pulled up to his middle. His muscular shoulders and tanned chest were bare.

So, undoubtedly, was the rest of him.

Bel sat up with a jerk. She, too, was naked.

His appreciative gaze strayed over her and lingered on her mouth. "You're even lovely first thing in the morning with a hangover."

She pushed back the sheet and attempted to get out of the bed. The sudden movement sent her head spinning.

It wouldn't have been quite so bad if the man beside her had been the man she was going to marry, but for it to be Andrew Storm...!

LEE WILKINSON lives with her husband in a
three-hundred-year-old stone cottage in a village
in Derbyshire, England. Most winters they get cut
off by snow! Both enjoy traveling, and previously
joined forces with their daughter and son-in-law,
spending a year going around the world "on a
shoestring" while their son looked after Kelly,
their much-loved German shepherd dog. Lee's
hobbies are reading and gardening and holding
impromptu barbecues for her long-suffering
family and friends.

Books by Lee Wilkinson

HARLEQUIN PRESENTS®
1991—A HUSBAND'S REVENGE
1933—THE SECRET MOTHER
2024—WEDDING FEVER

LEE
WILKINSON

First-Class Seduction

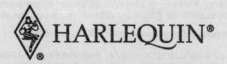

HARLEQUIN®

TORONTO • NEW YORK • LONDON
AMSTERDAM • PARIS • SYDNEY • HAMBURG
STOCKHOLM • ATHENS • TOKYO • MILAN • MADRID
PRAGUE • WARSAW • BUDAPEST • AUCKLAND

ISBN 0-373-18714-9

FIRST-CLASS SEDUCTION

First North American Publication 1999.

CHAPTER ONE

THOUGH lunchtime was almost over, the quiet back-street restaurant was still fairly full.

Bel Grant had just paid her bill and was preparing to leave when she noticed Mortimer Harmen, their company secretary, sitting at a corner table. In a reflex action she ducked her smooth blonde head.

She disliked and distrusted Harmen, and avoided him whenever possible.

Handsome in a beefy, florid way, his smile brash, his manner bold, he clearly thought he was God's gift to women.

He made Bel squirm.

Even during business meetings his pale blue eyes always seemed to be stripping her. The last thing she wanted now was for him to spot her and insist on walking back to the office with her.

A surreptitious glance showed that, though at the coffee stage, he was still deep in conversation with his luncheon companion, a dark-haired man who had his back to Bel.

She picked up her bag, and was making her way to the door when, out of the corner of her eye, she saw Harmen rise to his feet. He appeared to be looking in her direction. Muttering, 'Oh, hell!' she dived into the Ladies.

While she waited for the coast to be clear Bel

checked her appearance. She hardly looked like a fugitive, she thought quizzically.

Mirrored walls reflected a slim, charmingly businesslike woman wearing a charcoal suit and white blouse. Her gleaming ash-blonde hair was up in a neat chignon. Her oval face, with its small neat nose and generous mouth, the clear green eyes perfectly set and slightly elongated, was cool and composed, and free of make-up.

Though her father owned the cosmetics company she worked for, Bel used few of their products. Well marked brows and lashes several shades darker than her hair, combined with a flawless skin, did away with the need—except for evenings out or special occasions.

After hovering impatiently for two or three minutes, afraid she would be late for the two o'clock board meeting, Bel cautiously emerged.

The table Harmen and his companion had shared was now vacant, and there was no immediate sign of her *bête noire*.

Breathing a sigh of relief, she was making a beeline for the door when she cannoned into a tall, muscular figure and went staggering back.

Lean hands shot out and gripped her shoulders, steadying her. She found herself looking up into a pair of thickly lashed eyes the exact colour of woodsmoke, and was suddenly breathless.

Telling herself it was the impact that had robbed her of breath, she stammered, 'I—I'm so sorry.'

He said nothing, but as he studied her face a flame kindled and leapt in those smoky eyes.

An answering spark, a flare of excitement, of sexual awareness, ran through her, heating her blood and bringing a flush to her cheeks while she stood staring into his eyes as if mesmerised.

Then those handsome eyes blurred out of focus, and for an instant firm lips touched hers.

Drawing a deep, shocked breath, she pulled herself free and hurried out, refusing to glance back.

To any onlookers they must have appeared to be lovers taking leave of each other rather than total strangers.

She felt shaken and indignant, furious with him, and with herself, because she was forced to recognise that his powerful masculinity had appealed to everything feminine in her.

Trying to push the disturbing little incident to the back of her mind, Bel headed for Hyde Park, where the dusty trees and yellowing grass of late summer baked in the hot sun.

The offices of Grant Filey Cosmetics were situated in an elegant Georgian house in a quiet cul-de-sac close to the park.

'Made it in the nick of time,' the young receptionist-cum-secretary in the outer office greeted her. 'The others have already gone through to the boardroom.'

'Thanks, Rosie.' Bel smiled at the girl before making her way to the inner sanctum and sliding into her chair with seconds to spare.

It was a hot day, and Harmen, already seated, was mopping his red perspiring face with a silk handkerchief that matched his flamboyant tie.

At the head of the table, Bel's father, Peter Grant, a grey-haired, nice-looking man, his usually cheerful face set and serious, rose to address this emergency meeting of the board of directors.

'We seem to have a potentially dangerous situation

on our hands. Someone has already bought up a lot of our privately owned shares, and is apparently on the look-out for more. Whoever is buying seems to be working undercover, and all the signs point to the fact that it's an attempt at a hostile take-over...'

Bel, sitting on her father's right, already knew the disturbing news he was telling the rest of the board, and was aware that he was blaming himself for not having acted sooner to safeguard the company.

The previous evening, his brown eyes showing his anxiety, he'd admitted, 'It was a mistake to let Ellen keep those shares.'

Ellen, blonde and beautiful, friendly and ingenuous, closer to Bel's age than Peter's own, was his second and recently divorced wife.

At the time of the divorce Peter had been under financial pressure, and as part of the settlement had agreed to let Ellen retain a block of Grant Filey shares, relatively unimportant in themselves, but crucial in the present situation.

Trying to reassure her father, Bel had said with more confidence than she'd felt, 'Surely she wouldn't sell them without consulting you?'

The split had been an amicable one, and they had all remained the best of friends, but Ellen had no head for business, and what she wouldn't do out of malice she might well do out of ignorance, if approached.

'I wish I could be certain of that,' he'd answered, frowning. 'I'll be happier when I can get hold of her and make sure she doesn't.'

'How long was she planning to be away?'

'I don't really know. She just left a message on the answering machine saying she was looking forward to having a few days in Paris and she'd be in touch.'

Monitoring her father's face now, anxious on his behalf, Bel sighed. After more than a year of financial problems, he could well have done without this latest worry.

Now, as the meeting continued, her attention gradually drifted away from business matters, and she found herself remembering those extraordinary blue-grey eyes that had looked into hers.

With a shiver of something akin to apprehension, she recalled the flame that had sprung to life in their smoky depths as he'd studied her face, and her own instinctive response to that sexual challenge.

He must have been tall, over six feet, but apart from his eyes, and an impression of lean toughness, she had no real idea what he looked like.

Remembering the feel of his lips on hers, and still feeling flustered and angry, she went hot all over. Though the contact had been fleeting, there had been nothing in the least diffident about his kiss. It had seemed like a declaration of intent, a statement of impending ownership...

Oh, don't be ridiculous! she told herself sharply. It could only have been an impulse on his part. He'd seen a chance and taken it. Nothing more or less.

But the thing she found most incredible, and disturbing, was that a perfect stranger she probably wouldn't even recognise if she saw again had been able to affect her so strongly.

In an effort to banish the memory, Bel stared at the diamond solitaire on her engagement finger. If Roderick knew what she was thinking and feeling, he would be astounded.

Just the other night, when she'd called a halt to his lovemaking, he'd said, his smile a shade rueful, 'You always manage to stay cool and in control. Don't you find it hard?'

A little guiltily she'd realised it wasn't hard at all. She found it easy.

Too easy?

Concerned, she'd asked him, 'You don't think I'm really cold, do you?'

He'd answered, 'No, my sweet, I don't. No one with a mouth like yours could be cold. I just think you know the value of chastity, to use an old-fashioned word, and that makes you very special and precious.'

For a while Bel managed to keep her mind safely on her fiancé, but soon her recalcitrant thoughts strayed to the disconcerting stranger once more.

Scared of the effect that brief encounter still had on her, she told herself it was a relief to know they would never meet again.

Yet somehow, despite the fact that she knew he spelt danger, it felt more like regret.

When the board meeting finally ended, and the directors, talking amongst themselves, had filed out, Bel turned to her father and asked, 'Sure you won't change your mind and come to Kent this weekend?'

'Quite sure.' Patting her hand reassuringly, he added, 'I prefer to be in London in case Ellen tries to contact me... Is Roderick picking you up?'

'He's out of town on business, so as soon as I've showered and changed I'm driving down.'

'Well, you'd better get off home, then. See if you can beat the rush hour.'

'Promise me you won't spend the weekend worrying.'

'Indeed I won't,' he said, a shade too heartily. 'As

long as Ellen hangs onto those shares there's not that much to worry about.'

'You'll let me know if you hear from her?'

'Of course.'

The house Bel lived in was on the corner of a tree-shaded square less than fifteen minutes' walk from the office. Number ten Clorres Place, which was fronted by black spiky railings, had been divided into three self-contained flats.

Bel had the basement.

Having descended the wrought-iron steps to a paved area brightened by tubs of flowers and a long window-box overflowing with orange nasturtiums, she let herself into the small, white-walled flat and kicked off her smart court shoes.

After a cool, refreshing shower, leaving her long hair loose, she changed into a navy sleeveless dress and flat-heeled sandals.

These days she seldom wore high heels. Roderick was a bare inch taller than her five feet seven, and she had discovered quite early in their relationship that he hated to be loomed over.

Her weekend case was packed and waiting. She collected it and, after walking round the corner to a side-street which bore the sign 'Tenants Only Parking', got into her white Cavalier.

She was ahead of the Friday afternoon rush hour and her journey out of London was comparatively easy. While she drove she considered the coming weekend.

Roderick, an only son, backed by the Bentinck family money, was in banking. He owned a bachelor pad in the City but, having no great liking for town life, preferred to escape into the country from Friday until Sunday.

His parents, who were always delighted to see Bel, had given her an open invitation, and after she had become engaged to Roderick she had usually accompanied him.

Her father had occasionally been persuaded to join them on what, apart from the odd game of tennis, were essentially peaceful, relaxing weekends.

But on this occasion, because it was the Bentincks' fortieth wedding anniversary the following day, there was to be a weekend get-together. It was due to begin with a Friday evening party to welcome both visiting relatives and guests.

Bel had been looking forward to it until the previous day, but now worry cast something of a blight.

As soon as the Cavalier drew up on the paved apron in front of the mellow creeper-covered walls, Daphne Bentinck, a slight woman with grey hair curling around a cheerful face, came out to greet her.

'How lovely to see you!' she exclaimed as Bel got out of the car.

Defying the heat in a mauve twin-set and pearls, she gave her future daughter-in-law a quick hug before rattling on in her usual non-stop, staccato fashion.

'Roderick isn't home yet, I'm afraid, and I have to pop into the rectory. Such a nuisance. But you won't mind taking care of yourself, will you? You're in the rose room as usual.

'I've left the front door open for you. Leave your car where it is; Thomas will move it later. Tell Maggie to make you a pot of tea and some sandwiches to tide you over. Must dash...'

She trotted off at speed towards an elderly Bentley

parked in front of a stable block long since converted into garages.

Smiling, Bel took her case from the car and, leaving the keys in the ignition, made her way to the house.

As she entered the long, oak-panelled hall Margaret McDougal appeared and asked cheerfully, 'You'll be wanting some tea?'

'I'd love a cup. When I've put my case in my room I'll come down to the kitchen, if you like, and save your legs.'

As soon as Bel reached the pleasant, familiar room, with its rose-patterned wallpaper and light fashionable furniture, she unpacked and made sure the present she was carrying was safe.

A Jesse Harland figurine to add to Daphne and Roger Bentinck's priceless collection, it was simple and oddly moving—a boyish figure of a young girl in jeans, the head tilted slightly, the gaze shy but steady.

Roderick had suggested that, to get the maximum effect, instead of having it gift-wrapped it should simply appear on the Bentincks' breakfast table the following morning, and she had agreed.

Putting it carefully on the dressing table, Bel went to wash her hands and run a comb through her hair before making her way down to the huge kitchen.

On the oak table, large enough to have graced a medieval banqueting hall, Maggie had set out a tray with a freshly brewed pot of tea, a plate of dainty sandwiches and a selection of home-made cake.

'That looks wonderful,' Bel said appreciatively.

'Then sit yourself down.'

'Won't you have a cup with me?' Bel asked.

'Aye, I might that.'

Maggie filled two cups with the steaming amber liquid, and the women sipped in amicable silence.

Peckish, after a salad lunch, and with no need to calorie-count to keep her slim figure, Bel ate a couple of the sandwiches and a piece of cake. She was on her second cup of tea when the door opened and Roderick came in.

Though he couldn't be termed handsome, he was a pleasant-looking man, with fine brown hair, a thin, intelligent face and clear hazel eyes.

His small features, slightly sloping shoulders, and neat hands and feet made him appear somewhat prissy.

Which he wasn't.

He was open-minded, humorous, and excellent company, and Bel had liked him since they'd met at a business conference early in the spring.

'So there you are.' He stooped to kiss her cheek. 'I saw the car, and when you were nowhere about I thought you must have gone for a walk or something.'

Dropping into the seat Maggie had vacated, he asked, 'I take it you saw Mother? Did she tell you she's had to invite Suzy for the weekend?'

Without waiting for an answer to either question, he went on, 'It was a bit awkward, as her parents are two of our oldest friends. When they were invited, it was understood that Suzy would still be abroad. But she came home yesterday, and Mother had no option but to extend the invitation to her. I hope you don't mind?'

'Of course I don't mind,' Bel told him, while admitting silently that she would have preferred the other girl to be safely abroad.

It wasn't so much that she didn't like Suzy, as that Suzy didn't like her.

Barely eighteen, and spoilt rotten, the pretty, petite

redhead hero-worshipped Roderick and had been dev-
astated when she'd lost out to another woman.

Unable to control her tongue or her spite, she had
made one weekend visit very uncomfortable. Sensibly,
Bel had ignored all the gibes and, refusing to enter the
fray, had done her best to keep the peace.

But she wasn't looking forward to a rematch, especially with a houseful of strangers for an audience.

Clearly concerned that that shouldn't happen,
Roderick added carefully, 'I have every intention of
having a straight talk with her as soon as she gets here.
I'm fond of Suzy, we've known each other all our
lives, but I won't have you upset or my parents' anniversary spoiled.'

By eight o'clock that Friday evening most of the
guests had arrived and been made welcome, including
Suzy and her doting middle-aged parents.

It soon appeared that Roderick had been as good as
his word, for when the redhead, looking both older and
younger than her years in a black satin mini-dress,
joined the party, she gave her rival a small, tight smile
and then a wide berth.

Which suited Bel just fine.

Wearing a white dress with shoestring straps and a
full skirt, her flawless skin a pale gold, her ash-blonde
hair in a shining coil on top of her head, Bel looked
lovely—cool and elegant and poised.

Her fiancé, debonair in evening dress, showed her
off to his friends and members of the family she hadn't
yet met with undisguised pride.

A serve-yourself bar and buffet had been set up in
the large conservatory and, the evening being fine and
warm, there was dancing on the lantern-lit terrace.

Bel was busy enjoying the evening, and with the

party atmosphere drinking more champagne than she was used to, when she felt an uncomfortable prickle of awareness, and sensed that someone was watching her.

Lifting her gleaming head, she glanced around.

A short distance away, his back to the light, a tall, well-built man in immaculate evening dress was standing, his eyes fixed on her.

She saw his hair was crisp and dark, but his face was in shadow. Even so, she was sure there was something about him...something oddly familiar...

As the thought crossed her mind his white teeth flashed in a smile. 'How nice to see you again so soon.' His voice was low and intimate, slightly husky. 'Come and dance with me.'

Before Bel could gather her scattered wits, he had drawn her into the throng of dancers.

He was a good six inches taller than she was, Bel noted abstractedly, with shoulders wide as a barn door and narrow hips.

'I really don't...' The protest died on her lips as they moved into the light and she saw his handsome, strong-boned face, with its chiselled mouth, well-marked brows and thickly-lashed eyes.

Eyes that, ever since they'd looked into hers that lunchtime, had haunted her.

Though she felt as if she'd fallen down a lift shaft, somehow her legs kept moving to the rhythm of the slow foxtrot. In a strangled voice, she exclaimed, 'You! What are you doing here?'

He looked sardonically amused. 'I was invited.'

'Your being here is too much of a coincidence.' Gazing into that lean, compellingly attractive face, she spoke her confused thoughts aloud.

'Not at all,' he corrected calmly. 'Our meeting in the

restaurant was a coincidence. This one was carefully planned.'

'I really don't know what you mean...' What had been intended as a cool put-down somehow sounded merely petulant. Taking a deep breath, she went on more hardily, 'But I do know you have no right to kiss me like—'

He bent and covered her mouth with his, stopping the indignant flow of words and sending her head spinning. 'Like that?'

His kiss, though brief, had been shattering, and even when her lips were free again, her head continued to spin for a moment.

As it cleared she caught a glimpse of Suzy's startled gaze fixed on her, before the redhead and her partner were lost amongst the other dancers.

Scared, both of this man's arrogant demonstration of possessiveness and her own helpless reaction to it, Bel stopped dancing and made an effort to pull herself free.

He merely tightened his hold.

'Let me go,' she said in a fierce undertone.

'I want to talk to you. But first we'll get away from this crowd.'

Clasping her right wrist, he led her down the terrace steps and across the smooth expanse of gently sloping lawn to a wooden bench beyond the range of the lanterns.

She should have resisted, even if it meant making a scene, but, knocked completely off balance, her common sense swamped by too much champagne, she found herself going without further protest.

It was a glorious evening—the sky a clear dark blue pricked with stars, a pale, shining disc of moon hanging like an angel's cradle just above the treetops. The air was warm, soft as velvet, perfumed with honeysuckle and gillyflowers and the sharper, lemony scent of geraniums.

But, finding it difficult to breathe, all Bel was conscious of was the man who was holding her so lightly but inexorably.

Sitting on the bench, he drew her down beside him.

In spite of the background of lights and music, she felt curiously alone, isolated, as if no one else existed.

His handsome eyes silver in the moonlight, her captor studied her face with an unnerving scrutiny.

His long fingers still held her wrist and, knowing he must be aware of her racing pulse, she strove for calm. But her usual self-possession had deserted her entirely.

As though he knew exactly how he affected her, and was pleased, he smiled and said softly, 'Without that air of cool composure you're even more bewitching.'

Ignoring the compliment, she demanded, 'Who *are* you?' and was annoyed to find she sounded as agitated as she felt. 'Are you a friend of Roderick's?'

'A business acquaintance...Andrew Storm.'

'Andrew Storm,' she repeated slowly. 'Somehow it suits you.' Once again she spoke her thoughts aloud.

'And your name suits you, *ma belle*.'

Wondering how he knew her name, presuming Roderick must have mentioned it, she shook her head. 'I was christened Annabel, but it was always shortened to Bel.'

His free hand came up to touch her cheek. Flinching away from that caressing touch, and trying desperately to find some stable ground, she said jerkily, 'I'm Roderick's fiancée. We're getting married in October.'

'Really?' He sounded as if he doubted it.

To add weight to the declaration, she lifted her left hand and displayed her engagement ring.

'Why did you choose a diamond?'

'I didn't. Roderick chose it.'

With a shake of his head, Andrew Storm dismissed the solitaire. 'A diamond is too cold. You need the warmth of a topaz, or the green fire of an emerald. Beneath that air of cool reserve there's a passionate woman…'

Startled by his assertion, striving to sound amused, derisive, she queried, 'Do you think so?'

His arm went around her. 'Would you like me to prove it, Bel?'

'No!'

'Scared?'

Terrified. 'No, I'm not scared. But I *am* Roderick's fiancée.'

He shrugged, discounting the fact as coolly as he'd discounted the ring. 'So you've just told me. How long have you been engaged?'

'Three months.'

'Do you and Bentinck sleep together?'

The question took her by surprise. 'That's none of your business,' she said indignantly.

'It could be relevant to our discussion,' he pointed out coolly. 'If you *do*—'

'We *don't*.' The moment the words were out she could have bitten her tongue, realising she'd fallen into his trap.

He laughed softly at her discomfort.

Knowing she must put an end to this dangerous tête-à-tête, she gathered herself and, jumping to her feet, said abruptly, 'I'd like to go back to the party.'

Rather to her surprise he rose and, with an air of

satisfaction, as though he'd achieved his object, agreed, 'Very well.'

Tucking her hand through his arm, he walked her back to the terrace, where lantern-light took the place of moonlight and the party was still going strong.

There was no sign of Roderick.

'Have you eaten yet?' Andrew Storm queried, steering her to one of the small empty tables.

Her only wish to get away, she shook her head. 'I'm not hungry.' A shade desperately, she added, 'In fact I'm about ready for bed. I didn't get much sleep last night.'

As though he knew exactly what had kept her awake and restless, Bel's companion suggested smoothly, 'Worried about something?'

Apart from the few who *had* to know, her father wanted news of any attempted take-over kept under wraps. Hurriedly she shook her head. 'I expect it was this heatwave. I'm hot now...'

'Then I'll get you a drink. Some champagne perhaps?'

The thought of a drink was welcome, but she was not a lover of alcohol and she'd had more than enough for one night. 'I'd prefer a fruit juice, please.'

Watching his broad back disappear into the throng, Bel cursed the ingrained good manners that had prevented her from saying a firm no thank you, and walking away.

Though she could come to no harm here, in the midst of all these people, Andrew Storm was the most disturbing, *dangerous* man she had ever met, and she felt wrung out.

One of the guests she'd been chatting to earlier said,

'Roderick has been looking for you. He wondered if you'd gone to bed.'

'Oh...' Bel felt herself flushing. 'I've been in the garden. Perhaps I'd better go and find him.'

But even as she started to rise Andrew Storm was back, carrying a jug of iced fruit juice and two glasses, which he proceeded to fill.

'I chose the tropical. I hope that's all right?'

'Oh, yes, fine, thank you.' The concoction was cool and refreshing, and she drank thirstily before remarking, 'Something tastes quite strong.'

Taking a sip of his own, he considered. 'The mango? Or possibly the lime?'

'I'm not sure.' Finishing the juice, she said awkwardly, 'Well, I'd better go, Roderick has been looking for me.'

Andrew refilled her glass. 'There's quite a crowd still milling about, but if you sit here for a while he's bound to find you. Or are you scared of me?'

'Why on earth should I be?' She managed to sound coolly amused.

He smiled a little, but said nothing.

Picking up her glass, she remarked, 'You said you were a business acquaintance of Roderick's...'

Having accepted the challenge, it seemed safer to take the initiative and make polite conversation while they finished their drinks. Then, if Roderick hadn't appeared, she could go in search of him without losing face.

'Do you live in London?'

'I have an apartment on Park Lane,' Andrew Storm answered smoothly.

If he lived on Park Lane he certainly had money. Lots of money. Was it possible to be wealthy, successful, stunningly attractive and still single at his age? He must be in his early thirties...

'Are you married?' The question was out before she could prevent it.

'Is that a proposal?' he enquired interestedly.

Feeling gauche, and cursing her wayward tongue, she said as calmly as possible, 'As you well know, I intend to marry Roderick.'

'Pity. I'm firmly convinced that you and I are much better suited... And, in case you want to change your mind, I'm not married and never have been.'

In no mood for jokes, starting to feel a bit dizzy, she made an effort to gather her wits and get back on track. 'Are you a banker?'

'I own a merchant bank. Though I would class myself as a businessman rather than a banker.'

'What line of business are you in?'

'You could say I have varied and worldwide interests.'

She watched while he topped up her glass again, and, her words slightly slurred, asked, 'Such as?'

His excellent teeth gleamed in a smile. 'An oil well in Texas, a champagne house at Épernay, an opal mine in Coober Pedy, and an electronics company just outside Rome... Amongst other things.'

'How interesting.' For some reason she found it difficult to get her tongue round the word 'interesting', and her head began to droop, too heavy for her slender neck.

'You're looking rather tired,' he observed solicitously.

Enunciating with great care, she said, 'I *am* tired.' Swallowing the last of her drink, she rose unsteadily. 'Must say goodnight to Roderick...'

Andrew was on his feet and by her side. 'He's no-where to be seen. Neither are our host and hostess.'

'Oh…' She swayed a little.

He put a steadying arm around her waist. 'I was thinking of turning in myself. I'll see you upstairs. Which room are you in?'

'The rose room.'

'Ah… That's convenient. I'm in the jasmine room, which I believe is just next door.'

Blinking at him owlishly, she asked, 'Are you staying the weekend?'

'I'm staying for tonight, at least. If everything goes according to plan I shall probably leave for town in the morning…'

As he spoke he was steering her through the remaining revellers and, proving his familiarity with the house, taking the shortest way up the back stairs.

Opening her bedroom door, he paused, half supporting her, and bent to cover her mouth with his. Tiredness rolling over her in dizzying waves, washing away all her inhibitions, she clung to him while he kissed her.

She was still clinging blindly to him when he raised his head and, unwinding her arms from around his neck, pushed her gently into the rose room.

CHAPTER TWO

BEL came back to consciousness slowly, painfully, mouth desert-dry, head pounding like a trip-hammer.

Unwilling to wake, reluctant to face the day, she kept her eyes closed tightly. Surely it wasn't morning yet?

But it was undoubtedly morning. She could see the sunlight like a red haze and feel the warmth on her face and eyelids.

While her brain stirred into confused life her eyes remained shut against the light that threatened to dazzle her.

She felt terrible! Headachy and nauseous.

Was she suffering from flu? A migraine?

Whichever, and though proud of her full attendance record, she seriously doubted if she could make it into work today.

Maybe it was a weekend? she thought hopefully.

An attempt to remember proved unsuccessful. She hadn't the faintest notion what day it was.

Had she felt ill the previous evening?

With no recollection of the previous evening, or of going to bed, she couldn't answer that.

But wasn't she at the Bentincks'? Wasn't it their ruby wedding anniversary?

Yes, there had been a Friday night party... Dancing... Champagne... Too much champagne? She didn't drink much as a rule...

It had been silly of her to drink more than one glass of champagne on an empty stomach, but she had never envisaged such drastic results.

So how *had* she got to bed?

Perhaps Roderick had rescued her? She only hoped her state hadn't been too obvious. While he was broad-minded where other people were concerned, he wouldn't like his fiancée making a spectacle of herself in front of his parents' guests.

Nor would she!

The thought that she might have looked or acted inebriated made her feel even worse, and she moaned aloud.

'Feeling rough?' a sympathetic male voice asked, close to her ear.

Her eyes flew open.

Blinded by the sun streaming through the window, for a moment Bel could see nothing but brightness, then, as her vision adjusted, a lean, attractive face, the jaw rough with morning stubble, came into focus.

His brows were well-marked, his nose strong, almost aquiline, and above a squarish chin he had the most beautiful mouth she'd ever seen on a man.

He was lying beside her, propped on one elbow, a sheet pulled up to his middle. His muscular shoulders and tanned chest, with its sprinkling of crisp dark hair, were bare.

So, undoubtedly, was the rest of him.

As she gaped brilliant eyes between thick, sooty lashes smiled into hers.

Bel sat up with a jerk. She too was naked, her pale, silky hair tumbling over smooth shoulders and small, beautifully shaped pink-tipped breasts.

His appreciative gaze strayed over her and lingered

on her mouth. 'You're even lovely first thing in the morning with a hangover.' He leaned closer, as if to kiss her.

She recoiled and, pushing back the sheet, attempted to get out of bed. The sudden movement sent her head spinning and made her sink back against the pillows with a groan.

It wouldn't have been quite so bad if the man beside her had been the man she was going to marry, but for it to be Andrew Storm…!

The full horror of the situation was just beginning to dawn on her when, without warning, the bedroom door was flung open, and Suzy, wearing a short tennis dress, erupted into the room, Roderick at her heels.

'There! What did I tell you?' No one could have doubted the redhead's malicious triumph, while Roderick, still in his maroon cotton pyjamas, stood as if stunned, his eyes popping, his jaw slack.

There was a terrible silence before, his voice anguished, Roderick demanded of Bel, 'How *could* you?'

When, her oval face white as paper, her throat blocked, she only stared at him in abject misery, a hard flush of colour appeared along his cheekbones and he cried furiously, 'Get out! Go on, get out of my parents' house, the pair of you!'

He was turning to follow Suzy when Andrew said calmly, 'Just a minute.' Reaching across Bel, his arm brushing her bare breasts, he picked up an object from the bedside cabinet and, a look of quiet satisfaction on his dark face, tossed it across to the other man. 'You'd better have this back.'

Only when Bel looked from the glittering object in Roderick's palm to her own bare hand did she realise it was her engagement ring. She must have taken it off, sober enough to feel *some* sense of shame.

Thrusting the ring into his pocket, Roderick had swung on his heel when he caught sight of the Jesse Harland figurine on the dressing table.

As he picked it up, guessing his intention, Bel cried in horror, 'Oh, no! Please don't!'

But, ignoring her appeal, he hurled it savagely against the wall, shattering it into a dozen pieces.

Covering her face with her hands, Bel burst into tears just as the door slammed shut behind him.

As though it was the most natural thing in the world, Andrew took her in his arms and held her close, cradling her head against his broad chest while she wept unrestrainedly.

For a while her response to his tenderness, to the strength of his arms and the soothing murmur of his low, attractive voice, was total.

Then, horrified by the dawning realisation that she was accepting comfort from the man who, by taking advantage of her stupidity, was largely responsible for the situation, she managed to choke back the tears and wrench herself free.

Her pounding head protesting at the violence of the movement, she moaned, pressing slim fingers to her temples.

'You need something for that hangover.'

When Andrew swung his feet to the floor and reached for his clothes, even through her distress and discomfort Bel saw that his naked, bronzed body was lithe and graceful, with a masculine beauty that drew and held her attention and made her oddly breathless.

Pulling on his trousers and tucking his unbuttoned

shirt into the waistband, he headed for the door, saying over his shoulder, 'I'll only be a minute.'

As if he'd had the remedy to hand, he reappeared almost immediately, shaking a sachet of something that looked like sugar granules into a tooth glass half full of water.

'Drink that,' he instructed. 'It's not particularly palatable but it will lift your head and settle your stomach in no time at all.'

She obeyed, grimacing at the revoltingly bittersweet saltiness of the effervescent concoction.

Taking the empty glass, he added briskly, 'Now I suggest you shower and dress. I'll go and do the same, then we'll get the hell out of here. We can stop for some breakfast on the way.'

The very thought of food made Bel's stomach turn over sickeningly.

His glance knowing, sympathetic, he assured her, 'In an hour or so you'll be able to tackle a plateful of bacon and eggs.'

'I doubt it,' she muttered. 'I don't have that kind of breakfast normally.'

'Then you'll need to get into training,' he said quizzically. 'I love bacon and eggs, and sharing pleasures is part of the fun of living.'

Before she had time to take in and react to the mocking arrogance of that statement, the door had closed quietly behind him.

She stifled a groan. How *could* he seem so lighthearted in such an intolerable situation? Being caught in bed with his host's fiancée and ordered out of the house was hardly something to be proud of.

Yet he seemed positively triumphant.

Feeling like death, shaken to the core by the backlash of Roderick's anger and her own culpability, Bel stared into space with sightless eyes.

It hardly seemed possible that a weekend she'd looked forward to with such pleasure could have ended so ignominiously.

For a while she stayed where she was, her head in her hands, her mind in utter confusion, unable to untangle and deal with the immediate problems, let alone the wider implications.

Then, knowing some action was needed, she got out of bed and, on legs that seemed unwilling to support her, made her groggy way to the bathroom.

By the time she had cleaned her teeth and showered the potion was working and, physically at least, she was starting to feel somewhat better.

She had donned a cotton dress and sandals and was pinning her hair into a smooth coil when, with a perfunctory knock, Andrew returned.

He had showered and shaved and his crisp dark hair was a little damp. He was dressed in well-cut casual clothes and carrying an overnight grip.

'About ready to go, Bel?' he asked as she pushed in the last hairpin.

'I still have to pack,' she said helplessly. 'And I can't just walk out without seeing Roderick's parents and trying to explain…to explain how…' She faltered to a halt.

'How you came to sleep with one of their guests?' Dropping his grip by the door, he watched the hot colour pour into her face before adding wryly, 'I hardly think an explanation will help matters.'

He was right, of course.

Her voice sounding flat, beaten, she said with what

composure she could muster, 'In any case I won't be leaving with you. I've got my own car here.'

'My dear girl, you're in no fit state to drive. I'll take you back to town and arrange to have your car picked up.'

As he spoke he was opening drawers and tossing her belongings into her small suitcase with cool efficiency.

Zipping it shut, he put a hand at her waist and urged her towards the door, sidestepping neatly to avoid a shard of porcelain.

'Why did the fact that Bentinck vented his anger on the figurine upset you so much?' he queried, glancing down at the broken pieces.

Swallowing past the lump in her throat, she told him, 'It was a Jesse Harland original I'd bought for his parents. I thought it was *beautiful*.'

Andrew nodded without comment, then, taking both bags in one hand, he closed the door behind them and, an arm around Bel's waist, propelled her along the corridor.

Ignoring the back stairs, he turned towards the main staircase, saying firmly, 'Keep your head high. You've nothing to be ashamed of.'

If only that were true!

Her chin up, a flag of bright colour flying in each cheek, she allowed herself to be escorted down the stairs, across the hall and out of the front door.

To her very great relief they met nobody.

Andrew's sleek blue Jaguar was parked in front of the stable block, and in less than a minute they were purring through the pleasant Kent countryside.

Bel took in nothing of the scenery. Gazing blindly through the windscreen, all she could see in her mind's eye was a replay of her wakening to find *him* beside her, and the ugly little scene that had followed.

As though giving her a chance to come to terms with what had happened and regain her equilibrium, apart from an occasional glance at her pale, set face, her companion drove without speaking.

Just outside Mitford he stopped at the King's Head for something to eat. It was still quite early, and the clean, comfortable bar was empty. Bel took a seat on an upholstered bench in front of the open casement windows.

When he'd slipped off his corduroy jacket, Andrew sat down beside her. He was wearing a short-sleeved navy silk shirt, and his tanned arms were smoothly muscular, with just a sprinkling of dark hair.

He was much too close for comfort and, her breathing already impeded, Bel was careful not to let her own arm brush against his as they drank the excellent coffee.

Neither spoke, and, though conscious that Andrew watched her every move, as though trying to deny his existence, Bel avoided looking at him.

When breakfast arrived, Bel averted her eyes from the plateful of food set in front of her, her appetite nonexistent.

'Try to eat a little,' her companion urged. 'You won't feel yourself again until you've got something inside you.'

She was doubtful if she would *ever* feel herself again. But, realising he was probably right, she picked up her knife and fork and cut into a piece of crisply grilled bacon.

Some twenty minutes later her plate was empty, and she was finishing a slice of crisp golden toast and tangy marmalade while Andrew poured fresh coffee for them both.

Young, fit and resilient, physically she was almost herself again, but her thoughts were still in chaos.

Watching her face, he observed, 'What's happened must still seem something of a nightmare?' His voice was low and husky and sounded genuinely sympathetic.

But, unwilling to be dissected for what she told herself was his idle amusement, she said curtly, 'As it's a nightmare of my own making—'

He broke in swiftly, 'Don't blame yourself too much, Bel.'

'So who should I blame?' she demanded.

'Me, if it makes you feel any better.'

'It doesn't. If I hadn't drunk too much champagne in the first place...'

He frowned a little. 'Drinking too much isn't a crime. Nor is sleeping with someone.'

'It may not be a crime, but it's ruined Roderick's life as well as my own.'

'Rubbish!' Andrew said decidedly. 'My guess is that in less than six months he'll have forgotten about you. The possessive redhead will make sure he does.'

'She'll certainly do her best,' Bel agreed bleakly. And for the first time found herself wondering how Suzy had become involved.

Had the redhead seen Andrew accompany her into her room the previous night? If so, why hadn't she alerted Roderick then, instead of waiting until Saturday morning?

There seemed to be only one answer. Suzy had *wanted* them to spend the night together, wanted to be sure there would be no grounds for forgiveness or reconciliation...

And in that she had succeeded admirably, Bel thought bitterly. Not only would Roderick never forgive her, but she would never forgive herself.

Watching her expressive face, Andrew asked quietly, 'I suppose you must hate the girl?'

Bel shook her head wearily. 'No, I don't hate her. I can't even blame her for seizing the opportunity. Suzy's in love with Roderick and—' She broke off abruptly as tears threatened.

Andrew made as if to put his arm around her, but she flinched away, frightened of his touch, muttering, 'Keep your hands off me. You've done enough harm.'

His voice soothing, reasonable, he said, 'When you've got over the shock, and had time to think, you'll be willing to admit you've had a lucky escape.'

'A lucky escape! I happen to love Roderick.'

'Not passionately.'

'Enough to want to spend the rest of my life with him.'

'He's not the man for you, Bel.'

'In a minute you'll be telling me *you* are!'

'I don't need to tell you. Your subconscious already knows. When we bumped into each other in that restaurant it was like a spark set to dynamite. Then when we met for a second time that same spark was there, burning fiercer than ever. That's why you're scared to let me touch you...why our night together was—'

Alarmed by the undoubted truth of his words, and the feeling that she was being relentlessly taken over, she broke in derisively, 'Don't tell me...our night together was wonderful!'

Eyes gleaming, he murmured, 'So you do remember?'

'I don't remember a thing,' she denied, her cheeks growing pink. 'For all I know you could have raped me.'

'I didn't rape you,' he said quietly.

'But you did take advantage of me,' she accused.

'I didn't do anything you didn't want me to do...'

Knowing the strength of her reaction to him when her barriers were up, and guessing what it must have been like with all her inhibitions gone, she found herself reluctantly believing him.

'As I said before, you're a very passionate woman...'

Bel had never thought of herself that way. She'd had boyfriends since her schooldays, but a certain inborn reserve, a natural self-respect, had prevented her from indulging in casual relationships.

Throughout college, having decided on a career in business rather than art, a determination to succeed had kept her mind on her work when most of her contemporaries were paying more attention to their love life.

'How did you manage to hold out against Bentinck?' Andrew pursued. 'Or wasn't he that pressing?'

'Of course he was pressing!' she exclaimed. 'He's a red-blooded man.'

Andrew raised a dark brow. 'So in this day and age how come you didn't sleep together?'

'We wanted to wait until after we were married.'

'Both of you? I get the feeling that *you* were the one who held back. That you were never seriously tempted...'

It was the truth, and she was unable to deny it. Perhaps, on her side at least, that vital spark Andrew had talked about *had* been missing from their relationship.

'Isn't that so?' he persisted.

Cornered, she cried wrathfully, 'I don't want to discuss it.'

In no way fooled, Andrew smiled sardonically and observed, 'It would have been a very dull marriage.'

'How dare you presume that?'

Unruffled, he said, 'As well as being one of the pleasures of life, good sex is an important part of any complete and happy relationship.'

'It *would* have been good. We loved each other.'

'I doubt if Bentinck ever took your breath away and made your heart beat faster. He would never have been able to lift you to the heights—'

'I've already told you I don't want to talk about Roderick,' she broke in jerkily. 'And I won't sit here any longer and let you belittle our relationship!'

Only the damage was done.

Already Andrew had raised doubts, and Bel was even more furious to find herself wondering if she might have missed out had she gone ahead and married Roderick.

Contemplating Andrew's long, lean and no doubt skilful hands, and his mouth—a mouth that sent shivers down her spine—with a strange pang, she realised that she'd also missed out on what would almost certainly have been the most exciting night of her life.

But what was she thinking of? She ought to be mourning the loss of her virginity to a total stranger rather than the inability to remember the experience!

Oh, but she had been right to put him down as dangerous, she thought agitatedly. In less than twenty-four hours he had taken her virginity, wrecked her engagement, dragged her pride in the dust and, worse, made her doubt her own wishes and desires.

Confused, angry both with him and with herself, she said raggedly, 'Now we've had breakfast perhaps we can get on our way?'

'Is there any reason to hurry back? We could spend a pleasant day in the country.'

He must be joking!

As she began to shake her head he added quizzically, 'I'll do my best to keep my hands off you.'

With a flash of her old spirit, she retorted, 'Don't worry, I'll help you.'

He laughed. 'Then the answer's yes?'

'The answer's no!' The last thing she wanted was to spend any more time with him. She needed to be alone, to think. More moderately, but no less determinedly, she added, 'I want to get home.'

Appearing in no way put out, he rose to his feet, tall and broad-shouldered, overpoweringly male, and agreed, 'Very well... Would you like to freshen up before we start?'

As they headed into London, mingling with the Saturday morning traffic, he made conversation, forcing her to talk rather than relapse into a brooding silence as she would have preferred.

Avoiding anything too personal, he asked her opinion on a variety of subjects and listened to her answers with intelligent interest, sometimes agreeing with her comments, sometimes putting forward a different point of view that provided grounds for argument.

Roderick had never been one for debating issues, valuing women for their beauty rather than their brains, and Bel found the no-quarter cut and thrust of the present discussion invigorating and absorbing. She was surprised when she realised they had reached Clorres Place and were drawing up outside number ten.

But how had Andrew known where she lived? He hadn't asked, and she was sure she hadn't mentioned it.

Roderick must have told him.

Her *exact* address?

Unlikely as it seemed, it appeared to be the only explanation.

Or was there another, more threatening one? she wondered as, having surveyed the narrow, white-stuccoed, three-storey building, he slid from behind the wheel and came round to open her door. Was knowing where she lived part of some *campaign*?

Shaken by the notion, Bel was telling herself not to be a fool when all at once she recalled their conversation while they were dancing.

She'd said, 'Your being here is too much of a coincidence...'

And he'd answered, 'Our meeting in the restaurant was a coincidence. This one was carefully planned...'

Bel took a deep, uneven breath while every nerve in her body tightened in panic. Though she didn't understand how he could possibly have planned it, or what his motives were, she knew beyond all shadow of a doubt that he was stalking her, intent on taking her over.

All at once she became aware that he was standing holding open the car door, waiting for her to make a move. Avoiding his proffered hand, she scrambled out and headed for the wrought-iron steps.

By the time he had taken her case from the boot and followed her down she had opened the black-painted door and turned, at bay.

His smile slightly mocking, he asked, 'I take it you don't intend to invite me in?'

Ignoring what she recognised as a ploy, she said with cool civility, 'Thank you for bringing me home.'

'My pleasure,' he returned formally. Stooping to set her case down just inside the doorway, he added, 'I'll have Bridges pick up your car later this afternoon.'

'Thank you.' Remembering how she'd been welcomed on her arrival at the Bentincks', Bel's voice sounded hollow, and her face mirrored her desolation.

Watching her with his usual piercing regard, his voice casual but edged with an unmistakable concern, Andrew asked, 'You're sure you'll be all right on your own?'

'Don't worry, suicide isn't on the agenda.'

Hearing the bleakness beneath the flippancy, he frowned. 'In time things won't seem so bad.'

'You can save the platitudes!' she snapped.

Unruffled, he observed, 'It may seem a trite remark, but that doesn't prevent it being the truth, Bel.'

At the end of her tether, she started to close the door. Holding it with his foot, he said, 'I'll drop by tomorrow and take you out to lunch.'

'You needn't bother,' she told him sharply, too harassed to be gracious. 'I don't want to see you again.'

He spoke soothingly, as though to a child. 'Perhaps after a good night's sleep you'll have changed your mind.'

'No way!'

Smiling a little at her vehemence, he bent his dark head and kissed her lips. 'We'll see, shall we?'

A moment later he was ascending the steps with that easy masculine grace which seemed to characterise all his movements.

Though light, his kiss had had its usual earth-shattering effect, and she found she was trembling as she closed the door and leaned against it while she listened to his car drive away.

After a moment, knees still shaky, Bel made her way to the nearest chair and sank into it.

Andrew Storm had proved himself to be a determined man, and even if she kept the door locked tomorrow and refused to answer he could, and probably would, lay seige to the place...

Hands clenched into fists, she strove for calm. For the moment at least she was safe in her own home, and if he *did* lay siege to the place she'd just have to move in with her father for a while...

Her father... She groaned aloud. Somehow she had to tell him what had happened... No, she couldn't bring herself to tell him *everything*; he'd be too shocked and ashamed...

But she must tell him *something*. And quickly. If he tried to get in touch with her at the Bentincks'... Galvanised into action, Bel picked up the receiver and dialled her father's number.

He answered almost immediately, as if he'd been sitting over the phone, and she knew he *had* when he said, disappointment edging his voice, 'Oh, I thought it might be Ellen.'

'Then you haven't heard from her?'

'No, not yet. But you shouldn't be worrying about business matters while you're with Roderick.'

'I'm not with Roderick,' she broke in abruptly. 'I'm back in town.'

'Back in town? What on earth for? Surely you're not—?'

'I'm back in town because Roderick and I have split up. He has his ring back and our engagement's over.'

'Over?' Her father sounded thunderstruck. 'Are you sure it's not just a storm in a teacup?'

'Quite sure.'

'What on earth did you quarrel about?'

'Please, Dad...' Suddenly she was close to tears, 'I'd rather not talk about it.'

'Very well,' he said slowly. 'But is there anything I can do? You sound terribly upset.'

'Yes, I am,' she admitted. 'But there's nothing any-one can do. I just need some time to collect myself. A breathing space.'

'Then go away for a while. Leave all the hassle be-hind you. You've more than earned a break...'

She hadn't had a proper holiday since joining the firm, working all out to consolidate her career, and this year her father had several times urged her to take one. But Roderick had been already committed to an all-male sailing trip in the West Indies, and she had felt little inclination to go away alone...

Now the thought of getting right away was a wel-come one. Even more welcome than her father realised.

'Why not go to Rome?' he was suggesting. 'The flat is empty—' a pleasant second-floor flat was kept for any Grant Filey staff visiting the Rome offices, which were only a short walk away '—so you could see all the things you didn't have a chance to see last time...'

She liked the idea. Her first visit to Rome, after be-ing appointed European Marketing Director, had been a brief one, and there had been no opportunity to do any sightseeing.

'Enjoy the ambience—' her father was into his stride

'—and find yourself a spot of *la dolce vita*. Make it a real holiday…'

Recalling the other dark cloud that hung on the horizon, Bel demurred, 'I don't like the idea of being away with the threat of a take-over looming.'

'If I thought your being in London would make a scrap of difference I'd ask you to stay. But, as it won't, I'd feel happier if you went. So for goodness' sake go and practise your Italian.'

'I think I just might.'

'Now you're talking!'

'I'll try to get a flight out today.' All at once she couldn't *wait* to get away.

'Being Saturday, the flights might be full, so if you don't manage it we'll have dinner together tonight. Ring me at the office. I'm going in for a couple of hours. There's something I need to discuss with Harmen…'

After phoning several airlines, Bel was about to give up when she was lucky enough to find a single seat on a plane leaving for Rome that very afternoon.

Having no car, she rang for a taxi and, while she waited for it to arrive, demonstrated her state of mind by hauling out a large suitcase and throwing things into it with a disregard for order that would have horrified the old Bel.

Just as a knock signalled the arrival of her taxi, the phone rang. For a second she hesitated, wondering whether to ignore it. But it was probably her father. Snatching it up, she said, 'Dad?'

'No, it's me.'

'Ellen! Thank goodness! Where are you?'

'I'm still in Paris.'

'Where are you staying?'

'Hotel Colbert...it's not far from the Champs-Élysées. I'm having the most marvellous time—'

'Have you been in touch with Dad?' Bel broke in.

'Not for a day or two.'

'He needs to talk to you—' Another knock cut through her words.

'I'll give him a ring,' Ellen promised carelessly. 'But I *must* tell you about Jean-Claude. He's six feet tall and drop-dead handsome, with silvery blond hair and blue eyes. Honestly, Bel, he has to be the most *gorgeous* man I've ever met, as well as having the sort of manners you only read about...'

'Look, I'm sorry,' Bel apologised, 'but I can't talk now.'

'He's invited me to his villa at Épernay—'

There was a louder knocking and a shout of, *'Taxi!'*

'I'm sorry,' Bel repeated, 'but I have to go. I've a taxi waiting to take me to the airport.'

'Where are you off to?'

'Rome.'

'Oh, *business...*' Ellen said flatly.

'No, this time it's a holiday. And I really must fly. You won't forget to ring Dad? If he's not at home he'll be in the office.'

'No, I won't forget. How long are you—?'

As well as being a scatterbrain, Ellen was an inveterate talker. Hardening her heart, Bel replaced the receiver and hurried to open the door.

Less than two hours later she was on the Saturday afternoon flight to Leonardo da Vinci Airport, hoping against hope that she might be leaving at least some of her troubles behind.

CHAPTER THREE

HEAVY-EYED after a restless night, Bel sat on the flower-filled balcony and ignored her breakfast while she gazed across the sunny piazza.

Somewhere close at hand a dog barked, and, above Rome's background noise of traffic, Sunday church bells from all over the city called the faithful to mass, making what Bel, after her first visit, had described to Roderick as a melodious cacophony of sound.

At the thought of her former fiancé she had to bite her lip to stop the tears welling up. Poor Roderick. He hadn't deserved to be hurt and humiliated in that way.

Not even the fact that she'd drunk too much could excuse the stupidity and wantonness of her behaviour, and it was the realisation of what he and his parents must think of her that hurt most. There was one thing to be devoutly thankful for, though: she had successfully escaped Andrew Storm.

Refusing to consider why the unmitigated relief she should have felt was somehow mingled with a kind of unreasonable depression, she wondered how long he would keep calling at her empty flat before he finally got the message that she had no intention of ever seeing him again.

Probably not long. He wasn't the sort of man who would waste his time.

Despite the warmth of the sun she shivered, and,

making an effort to banish the image of that strong-boned, ruthless face from her mind, began to eat her breakfast.

As soon as she'd finished the fresh rolls and fruit pressed on her by Signora Paplucci, the plump, smiling wife of the mustachioed *custode di casa*, Bel tried again to ring her father but no one answered.

She'd also tried to phone him when she'd arrived at the flat the previous evening, only to find she was unable to get through because of a fault on the line.

By the time Bel was ready to go out, wearing a silky skirt and button-through camisole top with spaghetti straps, it was almost mid-morning.

Armed with camera and a map, she made her way down the cool marble steps, across the bare dimness of the entrance hall and out into the bright oven-heat of Rome.

Being Sunday, the shops on the Via Cordotti were closed, and the picturesque buildings, with their peeling shutters and flaking ochre stucco, had a deserted air.

A bus-load of camera-hung tourists, already pink and perspiring in the hot sun, strolled along the narrow pavements while pairs of local youths, riding motor scooters that sounded like enraged hornets, turned the smooth cobblestones of the roadway into a racetrack.

Bel was enjoying the colourful scene when a sudden wrench on the strap of her shoulder-bag made her stumble and fall, grazing her elbows and knees and sending her sunglasses flying.

Scrambling up, dazed and dazzled, she glimpsed a tall, dark-haired man dressed in fawn trousers and a two-tone shirt sprinting after the last pair of scooter riders, who were making off with her bag.

As he drew level he seized the man by the scruff of

the neck and hauled him off the scooter, which, after one drunken swerve, kept going.

The ensuing scuffle was brief but fierce. A moment later a blow to the jaw had sent the burly youth sprawling on the pavement and the tall dark man was returning with her bag. A man who was no stranger.

'Are you all right?' Andrew demanded urgently.

When she merely goggled at him, he repeated the question, stooping to retrieve her sunglasses and hand them, and her bag, to her.

Somehow she found her voice and stammered, 'Y-yes, I'm quite all right,' just as rapidly retreating footsteps indicated that the youth was making good his escape.

The passersby who had seen what was taking place and had stopped to stare began to walk on, and the next second it was as if nothing untoward had happened.

His eyes travelling over her with the proprietorial air that was becoming only too familiar, Andrew remarked, 'You've cut your knee.'

Removing a spotless white handkerchief from his trouser pocket, he crouched on his haunches to stanch the warm trickle of blood that was running down her slim tanned leg.

Staring at the top of his dark head, she wondered with a kind of stunned disbelief what he was doing in Rome, and how, in a city of over three million inhabitants, she'd been unlucky enough to run into him.

When he rose to his feet, towering over her, wide-shouldered and heart-stoppingly attractive, she stepped back abruptly, afraid he was going to kiss her, and, donning the sunglasses as a kind of protection, something to hide behind, demanded, 'Why are you in Rome?'

Apparently amused rather than annoyed by the manoeuvre, he asked mildly, 'Why shouldn't I be in Rome?'

'Oh, this is ridiculous!' she exclaimed. 'My coming to Rome was a spur-of-the-moment decision. You couldn't possibly have known...'

'Then you can't accuse me of following you.'

With a blinding flash of knowledge, she charged, 'But you *did*, didn't you?'

His expression bland, he said, 'You've just demonstrated that it would have been impossible.'

And on the surface it *was*. Yet Bel felt absolutely convinced that his being here in Rome was no coincidence. Though real-life coincidences could sometimes rival fiction, this one was just too bizarre to be believable.

'So are you trying to tell me it was simply luck that you happened to be on the spot?'

'What else?' His face straight, but his grey eyes holding a gleam of devilment, he went on, 'I noticed this slim, long-legged blonde and realised it was you just as the would-be thief struck.'

With that teasing look in his eyes he was almost irresistible. Fighting against the pull of his magnetism, she said thickly, 'I don't believe a word of it. I think you were following me.'

With exaggerated patience, he pointed out, 'I was coming *towards* you, so how on earth could I have been *following* you?'

Before she could make any further protest, however, he had tucked her arm through his, sending her pulses racing, and was walking her down the street.

'As it's still a bit early for lunch, I propose that as soon as we reach a café we have a cappuccino and sit down for a while.' Smoothly, he added, 'You must have had something of a shock...'

The worst shock had been to find that *he* was her saviour, she thought. And then knew immediately that *that* was what he'd meant.

Vexed that he was openly making fun of her, she gave him an angry look, and received a mocking grin in return.

He had an air of satisfaction, almost of triumph. Clearly he thought he'd won.

But she'd come to Rome to get away from him, and she wasn't about to let him take her over again. As soon as they'd had coffee she would tell him once and for all that she had no intention of lunching with him. Or indeed of seeing him again.

If she made her rejection decided enough he could hardly *force* his company on her. And, if he tried, all she had to do was jump in a taxi. He didn't know where she was staying...

Or did he? The thought raised the fine hairs on the back of her neck.

No, he couldn't possibly know.

He couldn't possibly have known she would be walking down the Via Cordotti Stretto, but somehow he'd contrived to be there...

She was still wondering agitatedly how he'd worked it when they reached a coffee-bar with red- and white-umbrella-shaded tables spilling onto the pavement.

Steering Bel to the nearest empty table, Andrew tilted the umbrella to shield her from the glare and, reaching over, calmly removed her sunglasses from her nose and slipped them into his pocket.

'You have the most beautiful eyes I've ever seen on a woman. It's a shame to hide them.'

As she blinked, feeling suddenly vulnerable, with effortless ease he secured the attention of a passing waiter and ordered coffee.

His Italian, she was annoyed to find, was a great deal more fluent and colloquial than her own.

Listening as he made the white-aproned *cameriere* laugh with a quip about the latest scandal spread across the centre pages of Rome's principal newspaper, Bel found herself wondering when he'd arrived. Obviously he'd been here long enough to buy and read a morning paper...

As soon as the waiter had moved away, she asked, 'When did you get here?'

A little smile played around his chiselled mouth, giving the impression he'd been waiting for the question, and Andrew answered, 'I flew in fairly late last night.'

Recalling her own difficulties, she commented sourly, 'I don't know how you managed to get a flight.'

'I came by private jet.' His voice was smooth as silk.

Bel bit her lip. She tended to forget that being wealthy he didn't have the problems facing ordinary mortals.

Though firmly convinced that he wouldn't tell her anything he didn't want her to know, she returned to the attack. 'You still haven't told me *why* you're here.'

'Would you believe business?'

Judging by his tone of voice, he didn't intend her to believe it.

'No, I wouldn't,' she said shortly.

He sighed. 'Pity. Then I'll have to admit the slothful truth. I'm taking what the Italians call a *vacanza*.'

She didn't believe he was taking a holiday either.

Though it sounded absurd, she was still convinced he had deliberately followed her here. But how had he known she was coming to Rome? Perhaps her father had told him? Though a little far-fetched, this had to be the answer.

The waiter brought their coffee, the pale froth sprinkled with chocolate, and a small plate of marzipan biscuits.

Taking a sip of her coffee, and setting the cup carefully back on its little padded doily, Bel glanced at Andrew and asked as casually as possible, 'How well do you know my father?'

For an instant a hard, almost angry look crossed his face. It was gone so quickly that she found herself wondering if she'd only imagined it, and he answered equally casually, 'Not at all. I know *of* him...'

Through Roderick, no doubt.

'But we've never met or spoken.'

Both his voice and manner convinced Bel he was speaking the truth.

So she was no nearer solving the mystery.

Andrew raised a dark brow. 'Why do you ask?'

'I just wondered,' she said vaguely.

When she made no attempt to elaborate, he coolly changed the subject, glancing at the map tucked into the back pocket of her bag. 'I gather you don't know the city too well?'

'No, not at all, really.'

Dropping some *lire* notes onto the table, he drew her to her feet. 'In that case, when we've had lunch we'll do a spot of sightseeing.'

His touch made every nerve in her body begin to clamour and completely scattered her wits. Like someone under a spell, she let him tuck her hand through his arm and start to walk.

So bemused was she, it wasn't until they'd gone a hundred metres or so that she awakened to the fact that once again, despite all her vows to the contrary, she was letting him calmly take her over.

Furious with herself, she stopped short and made an attempt to free her hand.

He wouldn't allow it.

'Let me go,' she began fiercely. 'I don't want to have lunch with you and I refuse to—'

His mouth stopped the angry words. One hand spread against the small of her back, the other cupping her nape, he held her close and deepened the kiss with a masterful ease that was at once passionate and punitive.

It was overwhelming. Devastating. Like being caught up in some maelstrom. Head spinning, she lost all feeling of time and place and her entire body seemed to melt.

When he finally raised his head, she opened heavy lids to find he was staring down at her, a cool, assessing look in his blue-grey eyes.

A split second later that disconcerting look was gone and, smiling into her dazed face, he was enquiring softly, 'Anything else to say? I'm more than happy to go on kissing you.'

From the corner of her eye she caught a glimpse of a small but interested audience, and, blushing furiously, muttered, 'We're being *stared* at.'

His fingers moved caressingly on her nape. 'I don't mind in the least.'

'Well, I do!' she snapped.

'I admit to preferring privacy, but if the need

arises…' glancing at a passing couple who were kissing as they walked, he shrugged '…when in Rome…' Then he added, his voice soft with purpose, 'Won't you change your mind about lunching with me?'

She hesitated, wanting to refuse but unable to go on fighting his determination.

He took her hand and, threading his fingers through hers, began to stroll along the sunny street. Resenting his high-handedness, his methods of persuasion, she remained silent.

After a time, Andrew glanced at her and queried, 'Have you been to Italy before?'

When she didn't immediately answer, he said humorously, as though determined to lighten the atmosphere, 'If you don't want to speak, just nod your head once for yes, twice for no.'

Smiling despite herself, she answered, 'I visited Rome a couple of months ago, but it was just a short business trip for my father's firm.'

'Yet you understand the language.'

'How do you know?'

'You obviously followed what I was saying to the waiter. How well do you speak it?'

'Nowhere near as fluently as you do,' she conceded.

Surprising her, he said, 'My mother was Italian, so though I was born in England I was brought up to be bilingual.'

'Your father was English?'

'Yes. He died while I was still at school, but, Anglicised by this time, my mother stayed in England instead of returning to Italy. After I left college I spent a number of years travelling in the more remote parts of the globe, and while I was away she fell in love with and married a London businessman.'

Then, harking back, he said, 'So how did *you* come to learn Italian?'

'Before I joined Grant Filey I combined a business management course with two modern languages.'

'Why Grant *Filey*?'

'When the company was first started, Dad had a partner, Conrad Filey, who dealt with the financial side of things while Dad did the marketing. It was a successful but somewhat stormy partnership, I gather, that finally ended with a quarrel and Mr Filey leaving the firm.'

'It must have been over something pretty serious to make him do that?'

'I don't know what it was over; Dad never told me.'

'What did you think of Filey?'

Wondering about this interest in her father's ex-partner, Bel answered, 'I never met him. I was away at school, then college, and he'd gone before I joined the company.'

'When you did, did you find any resentment amongst the staff?'

'You mean charges of nepotism? No, not really. Everyone was very nice to me. But because I *was* the boss's daughter I felt the need to work twice as hard as anybody else to prove myself.'

'And did you? Prove yourself, I mean?'

On the defensive, she said, 'When our European marketing director retired and I was given his job, I was satisfied I'd earned it.'

'How long ago was that?'

'Three months.'

That same weekend Roderick had produced an engagement ring and asked her to marry him. She'd been on top of the world; her career and her future had seemed secure and bright.

But now her engagement had ignominiously ended and the firm was faced with the threat of a hostile take-over. Any feeling of security had dispersed, insubstantial as smoke.

They had turned down a relatively quiet street lined with select shops and courtyard cafés when Andrew remarked thoughtfully, 'Your career must be important to you.'

Though it was a statement rather than a question, she answered, 'Yes, it is.'

'Then you had intended to keep on with it after you were married?

'I'd hoped to.'

'Bentinck's rather traditional. I can't imagine him liking the idea of a working wife.'

'He didn't.'

That had been one of the few bones of contention between Roderick and herself.

Andrew raised a dark brow. 'So, as the engagement went ahead, I presume you compromised?'

'Yes, we agreed that I would keep my job until we decided to have children, then I would devote my time to our family.' Stiffly, she added, 'But as it's no longer relevant I can't see that it matters.'

'I just wondered how strongly you felt on the subject. You see, I'm forced to agree with Bentinck on this. I don't like the idea of a working wife either.'

Before she could make any comment, he said briskly, 'But that's enough of work and business. We're on holiday.'

Bringing her to a halt outside a trattoria, he said, 'I'm glad you changed your mind about lunching with me. To get the most pleasure from life everyone needs someone to share the simple things—like eating lunch, a stroll in the sunshine. I hope you're ready to eat? This is Roberto's.'

Before she could catch her breath she was being led into the quiet unpretentious trattoria, where they were met by the plump, beaming proprietor, who greeted Andrew warmly and showed them to a secluded table for two.

After the glare of the street, the dim interior was curiously restful, the simple colour-washed walls pleasant and appealing.

'What do you think of it?' Andrew asked.

'I like it.'

'Good. You'll find the food is first class. I usually eat here at least once when I'm in Rome.'

'Do you come to Rome often?'

'Every month or so.'

'Always on business?'

'Not always.' With a glint in his eye, he admitted, 'I have been known to come for pleasure.'

The glint made her wonder if he had an Italian *amante* to provide that pleasure.

Finding the idea strangely unpalatable, but unable to let it go, she fished, 'Do you always stay at the same hotel?'

'When I come to Rome I have no need to stay at a hotel,' he admitted.

It wasn't what she'd wanted to hear, and she was wishing she'd let the subject drop when he added, 'I like to have *pieds-à-terre* in the places I visit most frequently.'

'Which are they?' She tried for the right amount of polite interest.

'New York, Paris and Rome, of course.'

'And you have an apartment in each of them?'

'I have service flats in the first two, and I own a house in Rome...'

Complete with mistress?

'Though I enjoy travelling, hotels can be lonely and impersonal.'

Even if he hadn't been wealthy, she felt sure that a man with his kind of sex appeal would never *need* to be lonely.

Recalling her own inability to resist him, she bit on the sore tooth and commented sardonically, 'I'd have thought there would always be some willing woman to share your bed.'

He heard the latent hostility, and the grey eyes narrowed, pinning her. But he said, evenly enough, 'While it doesn't suit me to live like a monk, I prefer to have one special woman in my life rather than a series of bedmates.'

A waiter appeared at the table carrying a steaming dish of Fettucine alla Panna, fresh Parmesan and, with Roberto's compliments, a bottle of chilled Orvieto.

The ribbon pasta, with its simple but delicious sauce of butter and cream, proved to be every bit as good as Andrew had predicted, but Bel left the wine untouched.

'One glass won't do you any harm,' he coaxed.

Repressing a shiver, she said, 'I've gone off alcohol.'

'You shouldn't let one unfortunate experience deprive you of the pleasure of a glass of wine with a meal. And we can't hurt Roberto's feelings...'

Seeing her waver, Andrew added, 'You'll find this Orvieto beautifully cool and crisp.'

A reluctant sip proved the truth of his words, and rather to her surprise she found herself thoroughly enjoying the delicate, fruity freshness of the wine.

As they ate she thought about his stated preference

for one special woman in his life, and realised that if the 'one special woman' *was* an Italian *amante*, she might be mistaken in thinking he'd followed *her* to Rome...

No, she couldn't believe she was mistaken. He *had* followed her; she was certain...

But if he already had a mistress, why pursue *her* with such determination?

Unless he fancied a change?

Surreptitiously she studied his hard face, the arrogant tilt of his dark head, the ruthless line of his mouth, the determined jaw, and, leaving aside the sheer attraction of those handsome features, knew she was looking at a man who always won, who always got what he set out to get.

All at once, frightened half to death, she shivered uncontrollably.

His quick glance took in that betraying movement and her sudden loss of colour. 'Is there something wrong?' he queried.

Giving herself no time to think, she demanded jerkily, 'I was just wondering what kind of game you're playing? What do you *want*?'

Thickly lashed smoke-grey eyes smiled into green. 'You know perfectly well what I want,' he answered chidingly.

In a fierce whisper she said, 'If you'll forgive the crudeness, thanks to my own stupidity and your lack of principles, you've already had me.' Then she blushed furiously at having put the main source of her discomfort into words.

His lips took on a wry slant. 'I thought I'd already made it clear that I don't much care for one-night stands.' Reaching across the table, he lifted her hand.

'And as far as *our* relationship is concerned, that's the very last thing I want.'

His mouth, warm against her sensitive palm, sent a shiver of desire through her. He was testing or enticing, she recognised, and she wasn't sure which. Probably both.

But, no matter how tempted she might be, affairs weren't her style. 'And the very last thing *I* want,' she managed thickly, 'is for "our relationship" to continue.'

Looking in no way perturbed, he touched his lips to the fine blue veins on her inner wrist. 'In that case I'll have to see what I can do to change your mind.'

Gritting her teeth, she snatched her hand free. 'After ruining my engagement and wrecking my life, nothing you can do or say will ever change my mind. As soon as lunch is over I intend to go my own way, and this time I mean it!'

'That's a pity,' he said mildly. 'I would have enjoyed showing you Rome...'

Having expected him to put up more of a fight, she was surprised into feeling something resembling disappointment.

'Ah, well,' he went on with a sigh, 'if our time together is to be so short, don't let's waste it fighting.' He held out a long, well-shaped hand. 'Truce?'

Unable to refuse the olive branch, she put hers into it. 'Truce.'

After a brief squeeze he let it go, and began to talk entertainingly about the Roman way of life while they were served a delectable ice-cream covered in toasted almonds.

As Bel took a spoonful a tiny flake of almond escaped and settled on her camisole top. Glancing down, she brushed it off.

Andrew's smoky eyes followed the movement and lingered on the soft curve of her breast outlined by the silky material.

Feeling her face grow warm, she kept her head bent over the sweet. Just his *look* affected her as much as if he'd leaned over and used his own lean fingers to brush the flake off. It gave her not only a new awareness of her femininity, but a disturbing sense of her own vulnerability.

Calling herself all kinds of a fool, she made a valiant effort to pull herself together, and by the time the waiter brought some creamy Dolcelatte and a pot of coffee she had recovered her poise sufficiently to be able to lift a calm face.

Having done justice to both the cheese and the excellent coffee, she sat back with a sigh. 'The whole meal was superb. Thank you.'

'Instead of thanks, spend the rest of the day with me, Bel.'

At this point in the game, she might have withstood bulldozing tactics, but the straightforward appeal threw her. She opened her mouth to refuse, hesitated, and was lost.

He read her unspoken capitulation and, masking his satisfaction, suggested casually, 'Tell me what you'd like to see?'

Throwing caution to the winds, excitement rising, she began to reel off a list. 'I'd like to see the Roman Forum, St Peter's, the Trevi fountain, the Colosseum—'

'Whoa, whoa,' he begged, laughing. 'There's a limit to what we can cover in one afternoon.'

She smiled back, the first natural and spontaneous smile she'd ever given him, and agreed, 'OK, so I'll settle for what's possible.'

Her smile lit up her face, and from being coolly beautiful she became wholly enchanting.

His eyes fixed on her, Andrew was silent for a moment before, reaching for her hand, he said a shade huskily, 'Come on, then, let's get started.'

CHAPTER FOUR

As SOON as they'd said *grazie tante* and *arrivederci* to Roberto, Andrew tucked Bel's arm through his and led her out into the heat of the day.

Noticing her golden tan against his own olive skin, he remarked, 'Though you're so fair, you seem to like the sun.'

'I love it,' she answered cheerfully. 'Which is just as well. What would I do on an afternoon like this if I didn't like the sun?'

'It could have its compensations.' Slanting her a teasing glance, he suggested, 'We could spend the afternoon in bed with the curtains drawn...' and chuckled when she blushed furiously.

Having hailed a passing yellow taxi, he helped her in and, sitting beside her, leaned forward to ask the driver to take them to the Roman Forum.

His muscular thigh pressed against hers, and every nerve in her body tightened while heat raced through her. Even when he settled back in his seat, he was too close for her peace of mind.

Intentionally close?

But he seemed to be innocently unaware of her discomfort.

Attempting to move unobtrusively, she edged away, and heard him laugh half under his breath.

So he had known! She found herself wishing that

she'd sat still and tried to appear indifferent, instead of making that revealing movement.

But either way he'd won, she admitted grimly.

The knowledge didn't please her.

Face averted, she looked steadfastly out of the window, but her mind was on the man beside her rather than the streets of Rome.

Why had she allowed herself to be put in this dangerous situation? He'd already proved he could overwhelm her senses, make her forget all the caution and common sense she'd thought an integral part of her nature.

Just being with him was playing with fire, and, having been burnt once, she ought to have learned her lesson.

But she'd had very little option. He'd more or less forced his company on her.

No, that wasn't the truth, and an innate honesty made her admit it. This time he hadn't used coercion. He'd *asked*. All she'd needed to do was stick to her guns and refuse.

So why hadn't she?

Now she was being honest with herself, the answer was frighteningly simple. Because he already had a hold on her imagination and her senses.

Deep down, in spite of everything, she had *wanted* to be with him, and, ignoring all the rules of safety and self-preservation, had weakly succumbed.

But, having faced the truth and admitted the full extent of her danger, she must remember how short-lived, how fickle physical attraction could be, and when the afternoon was over make a clean and final break.

That decided, she determined to push all the worry

from her mind and try to enjoy the rest of the day and the sights of Rome.

After a walk through the magnificent but melancholy, weed-grown remains of the forum, they made their way to the Colosseum, outside which, inside a semi-circle of tourist buses and flower stalls, several horse-drawn carriages were lined up.

'I thought we'd take a *carrozza* for the next leg,' he told her.

The black carriages were well-polished, the wheels and shafts painted bright red. Several of the horses were wearing straw hats, their ears poking through the holes, and she was pleased to see that they all looked well-fed and cared for.

She'd started to say so to Andrew when she realised he had momentarily vanished. He reappeared almost immediately and, dropping a light kiss on her lips, handed her a single, exquisite rose.

The nearest driver, his leathery face wreathed in smiles, gave an elaborate sigh and, putting his thumb and index finger to his mouth blew a kiss into the air.

Bel blushed as crimson as the rose, but, appearing in no way put out, Andrew settled her into the carriage and gave instructions to the driver.

They set off at a gallop, narrowly missing a bus, before dropping to a brisk trot.

To take her mind off the prospect of imminent death, she thought about Andrew, surprised by the things she was finding out about him.

Buying her the rose seemed to prove he was romantic—something Roderick had never been—and self-assured enough not to mind being chaffed about it.

She was lifting the rose to smell its fragrance, and

handling it incautiously, when she felt a sudden sharp pain as a thorn embedded itself in her finger.

'Ouch!'

Taking her hand and seeing the welling drop of bright red blood, Andrew put her finger in his mouth and sucked.

Desire, swift and urgent, kicked in her abdomen.

An answering flame ignited in his smoky eyes.

Heart racing with suffocating speed, Bel hurriedly drew her hand away and stared fixedly at the elaborate mass of white marble columns and steps that fronted the Victor Emmanuel momument.

'Romans call it "the wedding cake",' Andrew told her, only the slight roughness of his voice betraying that he was affected in any way.

'I can see why.' She was proud of the steadiness of her own reply.

When they reached the sluggish, weed-choked Tiber, Andrew paid off the driver, adding a generous tip, and helped Bel down.

'Ready to do a spot of sightseeing on foot?'

'Yes, I'd like to stretch my legs.'

Nodding his approval, he said, 'If you start to get tired we can pick up a taxi on the way back.'

For Bel, the remainder of the afternoon flew by in a kaleidoscope of wonderful colours and impressions, sights and sounds. It was almost six-thirty before they reached the Via Veneto, and walked up the famous street to the Villa Borghese, Rome's major public park.

The sun still shone, but it had lost its daytime fierceness and a cool, early-evening breeze rustled through the leaves and carried the sharp, resinous scent of the billowing umbrella pines.

Apart from the roads that traversed it, the park was quiet, and they had walked for some minutes before a woman appeared. She was preceded by a small, high-spirited boy running full tilt as he alternately kicked and chased a bright red ball.

His mother had just called out a warning when he tripped, letting out a bellow of anguish as he went sprawling on the gravelly path.

Before Bel could move, Andrew had picked the child up and was crouching on his haunches, talking soothingly, reassuringly.

By the time the boy's mother reached them his sobs had died and he was leaning against Andrew's knee, confiding that he intended to be a footballer when he grew up.

'Grazie,' the woman said gratefully.

As they resumed their stroll Bel glanced at her companion. She hadn't put him down as a man who would take kindly to children, and his reaction to the little incident, his genuine warmth and kindness, had surprised her.

'Hungry?' he queried, intercepting her glance.

'Ravenous,' she admitted cheerfully.

'Then we'll have dinner now, and that will give me time to show you a little of Rome by night before I take you home.'

The words 'before I take you home' rang a warning bell. Pushing the problem of how to prevent that happening to the back of her mind to be dealt with later, she mentioned, 'I'm hardly dressed for dining out.'

'You look fine to me.'

Instead of turning back towards the Via Veneto, with its many and varied restaurants, as Bel had expected, he headed further into the park.

Seeing she looked puzzled, he explained, 'I have somewhere special in mind, and if we stroll this way it should be easier to pick up a taxi.'

'Oh…so where are we going?' she queried.

He named a wealthy and select district beyond the Villa Borghese.

With the faintest stirring of unease, she said, 'But I understood that was a mainly residential area.'

'So it is, but it boasts some of Rome's finest hotels and restaurants, quite a few select shops and boutiques, and the best ice-cream bar in the city…' As he spoke he hailed an approaching taxi, which did a tyre-screeching U-turn and stopped beside them.

Andrew handed Bel in and, having given the driver an address she didn't catch, climbed in beside her.

This time, prepared, she had moved along the seat to leave a good foot of space between them.

He lifted a dark, mocking brow. 'Sure you have enough room?'

Determined not to be teased, she answered calmly, 'Yes, thank you.'

As though to punish her, he stretched a lazy arm along the back of the seat and stroked the side of her neck with his fingertips.

Her whole being concentrated on that light but sensuous caress, she was held in thrall until the taxi drew up outside tall, black wrought-iron gates, and he opened the door and helped her out.

Standing on the cobblestoned pavement, she glanced up and down what appeared to be a quiet, tree-shaded street of widely spaced private houses, most of them dating from an earlier, more elegant period.

Having paid the driver, who seemed in no hurry to be off, Andrew took Bel's arm. Opening the ornamental iron gates, he led her into a walled garden where a fountain played and a mass of scarlet geraniums glowed amongst tubs of dark green laurel and aromatic myrtle.

Guarded by gnarled cypress trees, the house stood sideways on to the road. Its walls were of ochre stucco set with asymmetrical windows, and its roof, adorned by turrets and cupolas, hung at unpredictable angles. Two ornate second-floor roofed balconies were enclosed by fancy grilles and supported by twisted columns.

'This is the Villa Dolce far Niente,' Andrew informed her.

Gazing at it in fascinated awe, she remarked, 'The outside's absolutely fantastic.'

'Then I hope you'll like the inside.'

As he opened the heavy door she hung back, suddenly suspicious. 'This looks more like a private house than a restaurant.'

'It *is* a private house.'

Realisation dawned belatedly. 'It's yours!'

Even as the accusation left her lips Bel knew she was mistaken. Any house of his would be functional and coolly elegant. This eccentric, whimsical, wholly charming villa wasn't at all the kind of thing a sophisticated man like Andrew would own.

But he was admitting that it was his, adding easily. 'I thought you might like to see it.'

Not on your life! It smacked too much of, 'Will you walk into my parlour?' said the spider to the fly...

As if she'd spoken the thought aloud, he murmured, blue-grey eyes gleaming with mockery, 'The closest thing I've got to a winding stair is a spiral staircase.'

'Too close for comfort,' she informed him crisply,

and wondered how on earth he could read her mind with such devastating accuracy. It made her feel both threatened and defenceless.

He laughed. 'Then I'll get Maria to show you upstairs.'

She would have baulked at the 'upstairs' if the reference to 'Maria' hadn't tripped her up first. 'Who is Maria?' she asked warily.

'My housekeeper...'

And mistress?

But he was going on wryly, 'A formidable lady who's capable of terrorising any poor male...'

Shaking her head, Bel totally rejected the image of Andrew being terrorised by any woman, let alone his own housekeeper.

'She *hates* anyone being late for meals, so I'd rather not keep her waiting any longer.'

'Keep her waiting?' Bel echoed blankly.

'She was expecting us to sit down to eat at seven o'clock and it's almost twenty minutes past now.'

Somewhat reassured by the knowledge that they wouldn't be alone, Bel was about to let him usher her inside when the absurdity of that latter statement struck her. 'That's ridiculous...' she blurted out.

For a moment he said nothing, but a sardonic smile touched his lips as he waited for the silence to suggest that she was making a fool of herself.

'How *could* your housekeeper be expecting us?' But now Bel sounded less sure of herself.

His voice full of sweet reason, he explained, 'Earlier, when we stopped for a drink and you went to freshen up, I had time to phone and tell her I'd be bringing a guest for dinner.'

Preceding him into a surprisingly spacious hall,

where a beautiful staircase curved in a spiral up to the second floor, Bel asked crossly, 'Why didn't you tell me at the time?'

He closed the door behind them, and asked with a glint in his eye, 'Why do you think?'

Because he knew quite well she would have jibbed at coming to his house to eat. It had been so much simpler and easier to make her believe they were having dinner in a restaurant.

Oh, but he was expert when it came to dissembling, to playing his devious games... Unscrupulous when it came to getting what he wanted. Prepared to coerce and, even if only by implication, lie...

She was about to tell him in no uncertain terms what she thought of his tactics, when a woman appeared at the end of the hallway.

Dressed in decent black, her grey hair pulled back in a bun, she looked every bit as formidable as Andrew had suggested.

Bel found the sight oddly reassuring.

'*Buona sera.*' The housekeeper's greeting was uttered with a thin-lipped civility that barely cloaked her displeasure.

Andrew gave Bel a comical 'what did I tell you?' glance, and said briskly, '*Buona sera*, Maria. I'm sorry we're late. If you'll please show Miss Grant upstairs, I'll be up myself in a moment.'

Without a word the tall, spare housekeeper led Bel up the curving staircase and across a wide, sunny landing.

Throwing open double doors into what was clearly the main living area, she announced curtly, 'Dinner is waiting on the balcony, *signorina*. If you would like to wash your hands first, there is a bathroom on the left.'

'*Grazie.*'

But, scarcely waiting to be thanked, the housekeeper was retreating down the stairs.

After a moment's hesitation, Bel decided that even at the risk of upsetting the woman further she *did* need to freshen up.

There were two doors on the left. The first opened into an oyster and gold bedroom, with a blue and gold canopied four-poster bed and billowing muslin curtains at the open French windows.

Closing it hastily, Bel tried the second, which proved to be a large and luxuriously fitted bathroom with another door leading into the bedroom.

As quickly as possible she washed her face and hands and then, noticing that the rose, which she had slipped through the clasp of her bag, was now wilting badly, she put it in a toothglass half full of water. Having fished out some pins, she ran a comb through her hair and twisted it into a smooth chignon, before hurrying back to the living room.

There was still no sign of Andrew, and Bel glanced around her curiously. The walls were painted ivory and the ceiling rose to form a dome, giving the room a cool, airy feel.

Furnished by someone with an eye for unusual and beautiful things, it held an eclectic mix of what appeared to be individually chosen items of interest and antiques. Only the comfortable-looking leather suite was unashamedly modern.

The doors leading to the balcony stood open wide, and Bel could see an oval table set with dazzling white linen, a centrepiece of fresh flowers and crystal wine goblets. Through the balcony railing, bathed in the golden light of evening, was a spectacular view of Rome.

When Andrew suddenly appeared at her side she jumped nervously, not having heard his soft-footed approach.

'So what do you think of my house?'

He had changed into slim-fitting trousers and a dark silk shirt, open at the neck, which clothed his toughness with an air of cool elegance and added to his already potent attraction. His chin was smooth, his hair still slightly damp, and she guessed he'd made time for a quick shower and shave.

Feeling at a disadvantage, she asked a shade tartly, 'Do you care what anyone else thinks?'

'Not as a rule,' he answered serenely as he led her out onto the balcony and seated her at the table. 'But it's the kind of house that one either loves or hates.'

'Would it hurt your feelings if I said I hated it?'

'No. But I would be disappointed. I'm convinced we're soul mates and share the same tastes.'

'I shouldn't bet on it,' she retorted crisply.

Having poured the wine, without waiting for the housekeeper to reappear, Andrew moved to a heated trolley and began to serve the meal.

'Gnocchi Verdi,' he told her, ladling out what appeared to be small green dumplings, 'Maria's speciality.'

When Bel had finished the last mouthful, she said, 'They were heavenly—the most delicious thing I've ever tasted.'

'Don't say that until you've tried the sweet.'

He produced two glass bowls of Tiramisu, some fresh fruit and a pot of coffee.

Sampling a spoonful of the delectable cream and

chocolate concoction, Bel murmured, 'Mmm...I see what you mean.'

'Maria's cooking helps to make up for the fact that she's seldom amiable,' he remarked dryly.

'Are good cooks hard to come by?'

'Not if one can afford to pay the going rate.'

Knowing she wouldn't have put him down as a man to suffer fools, or grumpy housekeepers, gladly, Bel asked curiously, 'Then why do you keep her?'

He answered simply, 'She's a widow with a bedridden daughter to support and take care of.'

'Oh...' Her thoughts skittering like pearls on ice, Bel queried, 'Does her daughter live here as well?'

'No.' He poured coffee for them both. 'Maria has a small house on the outskirts of the city.'

Since the housekeeper had hurried down the stairs there hadn't been a sound, and Andrew had served the meal himself...

In a half-strangled voice, Bel said, 'She's gone home...'

Though it was a statement rather than a question, Andrew answered, 'I sent her off in the taxi. But there's no need to look quite so alarmed. I'm not planning to spring on you.'

'What are you planning?'

'A pleasant evening together.'

'Followed by a spot of seduction, no doubt?' Agitation made her heart start to race. 'Well, you're wasting your time. I don't intend to indulge in a holiday fling...or anything else for that matter.'

'Why not?' he asked, suddenly serious. 'You want me as much as I want you.'

It was the truth and she was unable to deny it. From their first meeting the desire sparking between them had been mutual. But, though the flame burnt fiercely, common sense told her it could be no more than a passing sexual attraction.

'That's just a physical thing,' she said dismissively. 'What about deeper feelings? We don't even *like*, let alone *love*, one another.'

Unruffled, he suggested, 'You might grow to like me, or even—'

'I could never love you!' she broke in sharply, emphatically, determined to make it clear to herself as well as him.

His grey eyes ironic, he asked, 'And are you romantic enough to believe that no relationship can really succeed unless the partners love one another?'

Flushing, she lied, 'Of course not, but there has to be *something...*'

'You've already admitted that there's a very strong sexual attraction.'

'But if it's just a question of sex, why *me*? There must be plenty of women who would jump at the chance to share your bed.'

'I don't want "plenty of women". I want you.'

Frightened out of her wits, she cried a little wildly, 'But I don't know anything about you.'

'I think I can say that, apart from whistling off key and liking to shower *à deux*, I have no nasty habits, and my faults, though many, are relatively minor.'

Just the thought of that bronzed, muscular body naked next to hers in the shower struck her dumb and made heat run through her.

As if he knew, he gave her an amused, slightly taunting look that threatened to destroy what was left of her composure.

Somehow she found her voice and informed him

raggedly, 'If you were Mr Perfect himself the answer would still be no.'

Jumping to her feet, she added with what she hoped sounded like cool determination, 'So, if you'll please call me a taxi, I'd like to go home now.'

'Very well.' With a slight shrug, he followed her into the living room and, his broad back turned to her, picked up the phone and proceeded to do her bidding.

As she stared at the back of his neck, at the arrogant tilt of that well-shaped head, the neatly set ears, the way the dark hair curled a little into his nape, something struck a chord...

'About fifteen minutes.' Replacing the receiver, he turned towards her.

She looked hastily away, the fleeting memory vanishing like some wraith.

'Are you intending to hover until it arrives?' he asked sardonically. 'Or will you sit down again?'

Feeling safer on her feet, she took a step towards the French windows and, looking out to where the sun had lost its grip and was slipping below the horizon in a glorious blaze of crimson and gold, said mendaciously, 'I was admiring your view.'

Her strategy backfired disastrously.

He came to stand behind her. Iron bands tightened around her chest and she heard her own struggle to breathe as, holding her upper arms lightly, he drew her back against him and bent his head so that his cheek touched hers. 'If you look a little to the left, you can see right down to the Tiber.'

She stood transfixed, seeing nothing, aware only of the warm strength of that lean, lithe body, the feel of his cheek against hers and the cool, masculine smell of his aftershave.

If she turned to face him their bodies would fit together as if they belonged, two halves of a whole, male to female, soft curves to hard muscle. There would be a wild, singing sweetness, a *rightness*...

But she wouldn't. *Couldn't*. It was far too dangerous.

Swallowing, she croaked, 'The taxi should be here soon.' It was a prayer. Desperately, she added, 'I ought to go down.'

'Mmm...' he agreed, his lips brushing her ear. 'But not just yet.'

Bel took a shaky breath which ended in a silent gasp as kisses lighter than thistledown began to pattern her cheek and temple.

She was trying to find the strength to pull away, to put an end to this dreamy pleasure, when his mouth wandered to the angle of her jaw and down the side of her neck, kissing and nibbling, leaving little explosions of sensation wherever it touched.

Concentrating on what his mouth was doing to her, she was taken by surprise when she found one of his hands spread on her abdomen and the other lying across her midriff, his thumb just brushing the underside of her breast.

A sense of expectancy filled her, and her heart thudded hollowly against her ribs. This was madness, some vestige of common sense warned, but already the yearning to have him fondle her breasts was getting too strong to fight.

But somehow she *had* to fight it, to hold out against the insidious temptation of his mouth and hands. With a kind of despairing last-ditch attempt to defeat both his intention and her own desire, she bent her head and crossed her arms over her breasts.

He responded by taking full advantage of her vulnerable nape. The warmth of his breath, the dampness of his tongue, the sharp edge of his teeth as he half kissed, half bit, made her shudder convulsively.

'Please, Andrew, *don't…*'

As she spoke she realised his fingers were subtly removing the pins from her hair, but before she could get a hand up to stop him the silky mass had tumbled around her shoulders.

With a sudden, unexpected movement he turned her into his arms, strong fingers lifted her chin and his lips came down on hers, preventing any further protest.

Silently she resisted, putting her hands flat against his chest in an attempt to push him away. She might as well have tried to move Trajan's Column. He merely tightened his hold and drew her closer, trapping her hands between them.

She tried to keep her teeth clenched together, but his tongue-tip stroking backwards and forwards across the sensitive skin just inside her upper lip made her shudder. This erotic torment was followed by a series of light, plucking kisses that coaxed and invited, until she could no longer fight the urge to open her mouth to him just this once.

The exploration that followed was slow and sensuous, with none of the fierce passion she might have expected. He kissed her skilfully, persuasively, with no hint of urgency, as though they both had all the time in the world to enjoy the experience.

She should have been wary, but the unhurried gentleness of his kiss lulled her into a sense of security, made her believe she could bring it to an end any time she wished.

But when, fearing the liquid core of heat forming in the pit of her stomach, she tentatively tried, he took her face between his hands and, running his fingers into her hair and tilting her head to accommodate his wishes, forced her mouth to open more fully to deepen the kiss.

It was an assault on her senses that swamped any lingering caution and gave rise to a kind of drugging excitement.

Beneath her palms his shirt was cool and silky, but she wanted to touch him; it was a barrier. Without conscious volition, her fingers slid into the open neck to find the smooth warmth of his skin, the hard muscle, the slight roughness of body hair.

She was so absorbed that she scarcely noticed he was making his own voyage of discovery, stroking down her neck, finding the warm hollow at the base of her throat, smoothing her shoulders.

Not until he'd brushed aside the thin straps of her camisole top and slipped a hand inside to cup her breast did she realise the full extent of her danger and once more try to pull away.

But he wouldn't allow it, and her agonised whisper of, *'Don't, please don't...'* ended in a throaty gasp as his thumb and finger found and teased the sensitive nipple through the delicate fabric of her bra.

While one hand continued to drive her wild the other worked on her buttons, and a second later he'd eased the top from the waistband of her skirt and tossed it aside.

'The taxi...' Pulling free, she made one last desperate attempt to save herself, clinging to the thought as a drowning man would cling to a lifeline.

He cut the line with just a few incisive words. 'There won't be any taxi.'

'I don't know what—'

'There won't be any taxi,' he repeated flatly.

'You only *pretended* to call one!'

Making no attempt to deny the accusation, he drew her back into his arms, his kiss smothering any further protest.

CHAPTER FIVE

ONE hand held her against him and the other began to follow the curve of her hip and buttock while he continued to kiss her with an arrogant demand, a fierce desire that fanned the flames and threatened to send her own hunger raging like a forest fire out of control.

She was submerged in wanting, racked by the most devastating need she had ever experienced, when all at once he drew back a little, leaving her alone and bereft.

With a murmur of protest, she put her arms around his neck and pressed herself against him.

In a calculated gamble, he took her upper arms and held her away from him. 'Perhaps we should call a halt while we still can?'

'What?' she asked thickly, her eyes blind, the blood still pounding in her ears, desire running like molten lava through her veins.

'Tomorrow morning I don't want any regrets, or any suggestion that I forced you to stay. So if you want to leave, I really will phone for a taxi.'

From somewhere the thought came... He had already taken her virginity, so she had nothing to lose and what seemed like the whole world to gain. 'No.'

'No, what?'

'I don't want to leave.'

'Then tell me what you do want.'

'You know what I want,' she muttered hoarsely.

His face ruthless, he insisted, 'Say it.'

'I want to stay here. I want you to make love to me.'

With a little growl of satisfaction he swept her up into his arms and, like some conqueror, headed for the bedroom.

When he laid her on the four-poster, in the now dusky bedroom, she put her arms around his neck and tried to pull him down to her.

'Easy, darling,' he murmured huskily. 'While I like to see you're enthusiastic, I don't want to spoil things by rushing. We've all night ahead of us. I want to have time to touch you, to learn all your body's most intimate secrets.'

With maddening slowness he finished undressing her, kissing and caressing each inch of exposed flesh, finding all her erogenous zones, playing her, enjoying the way every nerve-ending quivered and responded to his touch.

When she was completely naked, he switched on the lamp and stood back to look at her as she lay motionless, vulnerable, open to his gaze.

Her beautiful hair was spread across the pillow, her eyes were closed, and he could see the rapid throbbing of the pulse at the base of her throat.

Slim and golden, her body was fine-boned, with curving hips and long, slender legs. Her pale breasts, their rosy nipples firm and waiting, were fuller and heavier than they appeared when she was dressed.

As he moved away from her she felt the cool night breeze that drifted in through the open windows, taking the place of his warm fingers caressing her heated flesh.

Lifting heavy lids, she found his eyes were roving over her, questing as his hands and mouth had been, and was suddenly afraid, alarmed by the way he was making love to her.

Like the revealing flash of a flare, it occurred to her that this wasn't how she'd expected it to be. It wasn't just a coming together, a quick and passionate exchange of sexual pleasure. It was as if he was taking her over, body and soul. Making her his so completely that she would never be free again.

She shivered.

Seeing that shiver, and misinterpreting it, he quickly stripped off his clothes and stretched out beside her, drawing her body against the long, muscular warmth of his own.

For a moment she tried to resist, to fight the sensual hunger that was keeping her enslaved, but before she could make any real move to save herself he was kissing her, and she was sinking, drowning, fathoms deep in desire.

His mouth at her breast made her jump convulsively.

'Please don't!' she whispered hoarsely.

'Don't you like that?'

'Yes... Yes... But I don't think I can *stand* any more.'

He chuckled softly, and said, 'My sweet innocent, that's only the beginning.' Then, having laved the taut nipple with his tongue, he began to suckle hungrily, tugging a little.

She heard the pounding of her own heart, and tried at first to swallow the little sounds and murmurs that rose in her throat. But the needle-sharp sensations were so sweet, so keenly felt, that she gasped and moaned aloud as the exquisite torture continued.

She was soon to learn that he'd spoken the truth when he'd told her that it was only the beginning.

His intense, yet leisurely lovemaking was like nothing she had ever experienced, or even dreamt of in her wildest and most erotic fantasies.

With his mouth and hands, and an expert knowledge of the female libido, he kept her poised on the very brink, enjoying his mastery of her body, until she was almost mindless with pleasure and with wanting, begging feverishly, 'Please, oh, please...'

Just when she thought she would die if he didn't soon satisfy the longing he'd aroused, he moved over her and she felt his weight pressing her into the mattress.

Though ardent, he was a gentle, considerate lover, and she was unprepared for the sudden brief tearing pain that, taking her by surprise, made her cry out.

As she stiffened beneath him he whispered, 'Bel, my beautiful Bel,' and began to kiss her deeply, passionately, at the same time moving with a careful domination that almost immediately began to rewind the spiral of desire, making her forget everything but her need for this man.

It was wonderful, awesome, this total giving over of one's self to another human being, this building up of sensation that grew so intense that the pleasure was terrifying.

She was mindless, lost to the world, her whole being intent, waiting, focused on that inner core of molten fire, her throat dry and tight from the gasping cries he was forcing from it.

Then all at once there was an explosion of heat and light that engulfed her in a burning ecstasy, making her whole body quiver and pulsate. It was so intense that it swept her up and carried her to the stars.

As she drifted back to earth, and her breathing and

heartbeat began to slow to a more normal pace, she was conscious of Andrew lifting himself away.

For a moment she felt bereft, abandoned, then he reached to switch off the lamp and, drawing her back into his arms, settled her head on his shoulder before pulling a lightweight duvet over their rapidly cooling bodies.

They seemed to share the same breath, the same heartbeat. She felt his fingers stroking her hair and brushing a silky strand away from her cheek, while peace, like soft black velvet, enfolded her.

Her last thought before she slept, was that he was much more than her sexual nemesis. Much more than her lover. *He was her love.*

Bel opened her eyes to find fresh morning air spilling into the attractive room, and bright sunshine slanting through the light muslin curtains.

Beneath the blue and gold canopy she was lying securely in the crook of Andrew's arm. He seemed to be still asleep and, afraid of waking him until she'd had time to collect her thoughts, she lay quite still, hardly daring to breathe.

Her first and only lover. Her first and only *love.*

The placid affection she'd felt for Roderick paled and shrivelled into insignificance beside the passion she felt for this man.

A passion that, rather than beginning with a seed of liking and growing gradually into love, had, she realised now, sprung fully formed into vigorous life at their very first meeting.

Yet how was it possible to feel so strongly about a man she was unable to trust? A man who, to achieve his own ends, had not only lied about calling a taxi but had tricked and deluded her into believing they had made love that very first night, when quite obviously they hadn't.

If she'd guessed earlier it would have made all the difference. Given her the will-power to resist him.

Or would it? a little demon of doubt queried. Just lately she seemed to have lost every ounce of self-control, forgotten all the principles and moral values she'd grown up with.

But, bewitched as she undoubtedly was, she had never intended to start an affair with him. It could only lead to pain and disillusionment.

Oh, why had she been such a fool?

A lean index finger stroked her cheek. 'A hundred lire for your thoughts.'

Jumping violently, Bel pulled herself free and leaned back against the pillows. Embarrassed by her naked-ness, she hitched the lightweight duvet up to cover her breasts and tucked it beneath her arms, before asking jerkily, 'How did you know I was awake?'

Andrew sat up, looking fit and healthy and incredi-bly sexy, his hair rumpled, a dark stubble only adding to his attraction. 'I heard your breathing change, and you were lying unnaturally still. So what *were* you thinking?' Seeing her bite her lip, he went on, 'At a guess, I'd say you were giving yourself hell for behav-ing like a warm, passionate woman?'

Her expression was answer enough.

He sighed. 'I was hoping you wouldn't wake up re-gretting it.'

'What else can I do but regret it?' she burst out, her green eyes agitated. 'I should have had more sense than to let you persuade me to stay...'

A wry smile twisted his lips.

Flushing, she said, 'I know you *asked* if I wanted to leave...'

'And you said no.'

'But then I thought—' She broke off, her colour deepening.

'That we'd already made love?'

'It was what you intended me to think!'

He made no attempt to deny it.

'You lied to me!'

'I didn't tell you any lies. I only let you believe it had happened.'

As she contemplated this fine distinction in silence he said plaintively, 'You were angry when you thought I'd seduced you, now you're angry because I hadn't.'

Though she knew full well that he was teasing her, she couldn't prevent herself answering crossly, 'I'm not angry because you hadn't. I'm angry because you deliberately misled me... Why did you want me to believe something you knew wasn't true?'

Just for an instant he looked disconcerted, then he said, 'Do you really need to ask?'

No, she didn't. She already had her answer.

Because she'd believed her bridges had already been burnt, it had seemed so much easier to go forward.

And he'd realised that would be the case. Banked on it, the swine!

But if he'd intended to have her anyway, *why* hadn't he taken her that first night? She'd certainly been in no state to resist.

Hesitant about asking the question direct, she said obliquely, 'I can't remember anything that happened after leaving the party.'

'I helped you upstairs and into your room, and gave you a hand to undress—'

Cheeks burning, she broke in sarcastically, 'How very noble of you.'

'Then I lifted you into bed.'

A thought struck her. 'And you took off my ring!'

'Yes,' he admitted. 'But apart from that I didn't lay a finger on you.'

'Why? I must have been far too drunk to put up any resistance.'

She saw his jaw tighten and knew the implication had made him furious.

His voice smooth, yet abrasive as pumice stone, he said coldly, 'I've always had a silly preference for my partner to be wide awake and co-operative. You were fast asleep as soon as your head touched the pillow.'

Curious enough to brave his wrath, she asked, 'But if you didn't intend to...to take advantage of me...why didn't you go to your own room?'

For a second or two his face became a blank mask, as though a shutter had dropped, then he shrugged slightly. 'Maybe I had hopes of...shall we say...an early-morning romp, when you'd slept it off?'

An early-morning romp? Somehow it didn't ring true. Yet what other reason could there be? 'Even though you knew I was engaged to Roderick?'

He reached out to brush the back of his hand down her half-averted cheek. 'As I told you once before, he isn't the man for you.'

'That's a matter of opinion,' she said sharply.

'Do you still imagine he's the love of your life?' Andrew's question made a sudden harsh counterpoint to the caress of his fingers.

She shook her head mutely.

He took hold of her shoulders and turned her to face

him. 'Tell me something, Bel... If Bentinck changed his mind and asked you to go back to him, would you?'

'No. It would be no use. In just a few days everything's changed.' Almost to herself, she added, 'I'm not the same person any longer.'

'Well, if you're willing to concede that, we're making *some* progress,' Andrew said.

His casual arrogance stung her, and she pulled herself free.

'How much ''progress'' were you hoping for?' Giving him no chance to answer, she rushed on, 'As far as I'm concerned last night was a terrible mistake and should never have happened, so if you were thinking of a full-scale affair, you can think again.'

'That's fine by me—' his smile was serene '—because an affair isn't what I have in mind.'

'Oh...' Bel was taken aback. She'd been so sure. 'Then what *do* you have in mind?'

With calm certainty, he informed her, 'I intend to marry you.'

'*Marry* me?' The shock was chaotic, literally robbing her of breath.

He couldn't mean it! Yet with every nerve in her body tightening with a combination of alarm and excitement, she knew he *did*. Both his voice and his expression had been implacable.

Cool, heavy-lidded eyes studied her face, gauging her reaction. 'What do you think of the idea?'

When she could breathe again, she said, 'It's totally absurd!'

'Why is it absurd?'

'We're little more than strangers.'

'*Intimate* strangers, wouldn't you say?'

Determinedly ignoring his quizzical glance, she pointed out jerkily, 'We only met three days ago.'

'By dispensing with the usual conventions we've come a long way in three days.'

'You still don't know me,' she protested. 'I could be quite impossible...'

'I know you're not cruel, vain, vindictive, empty-headed or shallow. Anything else I can live with.'

'But why *marriage*? I just don't understand.'

'Because I *want* to marry you. And with you having lured me to bed...'

Rising to the bait, she cried, 'I did no such thing!'

Ignoring her indignant denial, he went on ironically, 'I think you should make an honest man of me.'

Leaning towards her, he blew softly, watching a pale, silky tendril of hair move against her neck before asking, 'Hungry?'

Thrown by the sudden change of direction, she looked at him warily. 'For what?'

Eyes gleaming between thick, dark lashes, he murmured, 'I can provide whatever you need. Food, or...'

Swallowing, she managed jerkily, 'Make it food. Despite last night's excellent meal, I'm ravenous.'

She felt a strange mixture of relief and disappointment when, sighing, he commented, 'Not very romantic, but somehow reassuringly wife-like. Ah, well, as soon as I've showered I'll rustle up some breakfast.'

'Won't your housekeeper...?'

'I've given Maria the day off.'

Far from enthusiastic about encountering what she guessed would have been grim, if tacit disapproval, Bel could only feel pleased.

Throwing back the duvet, he got out of bed, and as

she watched him stretch, lithe and virile, the now familiar pang of desire clutched at her stomach.

Though he was tall, there was nothing ungainly about him. All his movements held the unconscious animal grace of someone perfectly co-ordinated, in control of his own body.

As though feeling her eyes on him, he turned to drop a brief kiss on her mouth. 'You can have the *en suite* bathroom all to yourself... Unless you'd like to shower with me?'

Her heart began to beat erratically and her throat went dry. 'No, thank you,' she refused hurriedly.

Sighing, he agreed, 'Perhaps you're right.' Then he added mockingly, 'I suppose we should save *some* excitement for when we're married.'

Shrugging into a short black silk dressing gown that had been thrown over a chair, he went out, closing the door quietly behind him, leaving her thoughts in chaos.

The whole thing was utter madness. But just hearing 'when we're married' said so lightly somehow made the idea more concrete. Made it seem feasible.

Thoughts crowding and jostling in her mind, chaotic as Rome's traffic, Bel got out of bed and made her way to the bathroom.

Miraculously the rose had recovered and, its crimson petals opened wider, was perfuming the air. Its triumphant survival seemed to be in some strange way symbolic, but symbolic of what, she wasn't sure.

When she'd showered, enjoying the flow of hot water over her skin, she dried herself on the soft, absorbent towels and borrowed a short white bathrobe which, though she was tall and far from narrow across the shoulders, managed to swamp her.

Almost as if its owner had expected an unequipped

visitor, there was a hairbrush and a toothbrush still in their cellophane packets, and an untouched tube of toothpaste.

After cleaning her teeth and fastening her long hair into a ponytail, Bel made a quick foray into the deserted living room to find her discarded top, before going back to the bedroom to collect the rest of her clothing, grimacing at the thought of having to wear yesterday's undies.

But the matching peach chiffon set had vanished, and lying over the chair where they had been was an exquisite satin and lace eau-de-Nil bra and a pair of dainty panties.

Though they were her size, she had never seen them before, and it was obvious that they were brand-new.

Flabbergasted, she stood quite still, gaping open-mouthed at them. How on earth…? Unless Andrew was some kind of magician…?

Closing her mouth, she told herself sternly that there must be a logical explanation for their presence.

A sister, perhaps?

No, he'd spoken as if he was, like herself, an only child.

So had they been bought for a previous lady-friend?

That seemed to be the most likely.

He had a nerve!

Gritting her teeth, Bel hesitated. It was a case of either borrowing the garments and dressing or confronting him in the terry robe, which, no matter how tightly she tied the belt, seemed to have a disconcerting tendency to gape open.

Deciding she'd feel more confident fully clothed, she gathered up the undies and went back into the bathroom to get dressed.

When she returned to the living room, which had lost its initial strangeness and was starting to look familiar, she found there was still no sign of Andrew, but an appetising smell of coffee wafted in from the balcony.

Heading that way, Bel saw he was already at the table, casually but smartly dressed, leisurely turning the pages of the morning *giornale*.

Tossing the newspaper aside, he rose to his feet at her approach and, with the courtesy that seemed to come naturally to him, pulled out a chair for her.

'Coffee?' he queried. 'Or would you prefer to start with orange juice?'

'Coffee, please,' she answered tightly.

His quick glance took in her grim expression, but he filled both their cups from the cafetière without comment, and she sipped in silence while he helped her to a warm roll and some delicious-looking cherry conserve.

The balmy air carried the evocative scent of pine and myrtle, and the sun, having scaled the vine-covered wall, was using the wrought-iron of the balcony to paint tiger stripes of light and shade across the snowy cloth.

Deciding to leave the bigger issue for the moment, Bel braced herself to deal with the smaller one. 'The undies I'm wearing, where did they come from?'

Appearing in no way put out, he answered casually, 'From a small boutique just round the corner.'

Her soft mouth tightened. 'I mean, who do they belong to?'

'Ah,' he murmured softly, 'I see. No, they're not some ex-mistress's. They were bought for you.'

'I don't see how they could have been,' she objected.

'The lady who runs the boutique happens to be a friend of mine, so I phoned to tell her what was needed. By the time I'd finished showering, her assistant had brought them round.'

Bel was forced to admit that most men would probably never have thought to question her needs. Andrew had not only thought, but taken the trouble to provide an answer.

Flustered, ashamed of her previous tone, she said, 'Oh... Well, thank you... But you must let me pay for them. I really can't accept—'

'As we're going to be married,' he broke in firmly, 'I can't see that one inexpensive gift is going to compromise you.'

'Who said we were going to be married?'

He studied her, slit-eyed against the sun. 'When you opted to stay for breakfast, instead of running as fast as your legs could carry you, I presumed you must have decided in favour.'

Perhaps her subconscious had? Terrified by the thought, she cried in panic, 'No, no, I haven't. I—I *can't* marry you.'

'Why not?' he asked calmly. 'You know you want to.'

It was the truth, and she was badly shaken to realise *how much* she wanted to. He was the only man who had ever succeeded in getting through her defences, the only man she had ever gone overboard for.

But everything had happened so quickly, and how could she consider marrying someone who felt nothing for her apart from a powerful sexual attraction?

Hardly above a whisper, she said, 'It would never work.'

The strong bones prominent, the dark brows sharply

accenting his face, he urged, 'If we were both prepared to try we could *make* it work. Any relationship, whether the people involved love each other or not, needs a willingness to give and take if it's to succeed.

'We've got a lot going for us. Contrary to what you seem to think, I want more from marriage than just a woman to warm my bed. I want someone with similar tastes to share things with, good companionship... Good companionship should be rated as highly as good sex. Wouldn't you agree?'

Disconcerted by his sudden question, she found herself stammering, 'Well, yes, I—I suppose so. But I still don't believe it would work.'

'Because we don't love each other?'

Not trusting herself to speak, she nodded.

'You look about fifteen with that ponytail, but you must be twenty-one or two?'

Startled, she answered, 'I'm twenty-three.'

'How many times have you been in love?'

'Once,' she answered truthfully, if misleadingly.

'Which proves you don't give your heart easily...'

If only he knew!

'You've admitted you wouldn't go back to Bentinck, and you're not the kind of woman to indulge in casual affairs, so if you don't marry me, what are you going to do?'

What *would* she do with her life? A future alone looked grey and bleak and depressingly empty compared with what she might have if she married Andrew.

His eyes on her face, he pursued, 'You and Bentinck had discussed the subject, so you must want children?'

'Yes, but...' She hesitated.

Usually Andrew kept his emotions well hidden behind a cool barrier of good-humoured sophistication, but now his jaw tightened with anger. 'You wouldn't want *mine*?'

Shaking her head, she managed, 'That wasn't what I was going to say.'

'What *were* you going to say?'

Swallowing hard, she ducked her head. 'I was about to ask if *you* would want children?'

'I'd always intended to have a family once I'd found the right woman.'

He would make a good father, Bel found herself thinking, as she remembered the child in the Villa Borghese.

Reaching out his hand, he lifted her chin. Recognising that she was weakening, he pressed, 'So it's settled?'

As if there was no help for it, she nodded.

Just for an instant a look of almost savage triumph flared in his handsome eyes, then it vanished. His voice casual, he said, 'In that case I suggest we fly back to London without delay and I'll make arrangements for us to be married as soon as possible.'

Feeling as though she had been snatched up by some whirlwind, she protested, 'Why the hurry?' Then, half-jokingly, she said, 'Are you afraid I'll change my mind?'

The instant the words left her lips she saw by his expression that she'd put her finger on it.

His face becoming suddenly guarded, he answered a shade brusquely, 'Let's say I can't wait to make you my wife.'

'But I need time. I have to talk to Dad and—'

'Time might be something we haven't got too much of.'

'I don't understand what you mean.'

Coolly, he pointed out, 'There's a possibility you may already be pregnant.'

As the matter-of-fact statement exploded inside her head like a hand grenade Bel realised he'd sounded serene, complacent, anything but concerned.

But he had *known* what kind of woman he was taking to bed, and he must have been aware that she'd been too overwhelmed by passion to give it any thought. So why hadn't a man of his experience exercised some caution?

The answer seemed obvious. He'd been hoping for an additional weapon to use against her, to force her into marrying him...

Jumping to her feet, she burst out, 'You *wanted* me to get pregnant, didn't you?'

Lean fingers closed around her wrist and jerked her onto his knee. When she would have wriggled free, a steely arm held her captive while his lips brushed her bare shoulder in a sensuous caress.

'I'm in no particular hurry to become a father...' His mouth moved up the side of her neck to the warmth of her nape, punctuating his words with a series of soft, baby kisses that made chills run up and down her spine.

Feeling her shiver, he went on, 'As a matter of fact I'd prefer us to have a few years on our own first, so you can travel with me and we can enjoy getting to know one another... But just in case you *are* pregnant, and to observe the proprieties, I think we should be married without delay.' His lips followed the clean curve of her jaw and lingered tantalisingly at the corner of her mouth. 'Agreed?'

Common sense warned that the old saying 'Marry in haste, repent at leisure' was most probably not only trite but true. But, though she might live to regret it, there was no way she could say no.

'Agreed.' Her whispered assent was lost as his mouth closed over hers and he kissed her with an expertise that sent the world spinning and blotted out the bright day.

When he raised his head, she opened dazed green eyes to find he was smiling, watching her in a way that made her skin prickle.

Softly, he said, 'I'd like nothing better than to take you back to bed and stay there all day, but unfortunately we haven't the time.' Then, in the tone of someone who is prepared to brook no argument, he added, 'You'll fly home with me, of course?'

Accepting that there was no way she could slow down the whirlwind, Bel nodded. 'Yes, but I'll need to go back to the flat to pack and hand in the key.'

CHAPTER SIX

THE instant his aims were accomplished, the ardent lover was replaced by a cool, brisk man of business. 'I'll ring the airport and let Captain Drummond, my pilot, know when we'll be ready to leave.'

While Bel sat over a freshly poured cup of coffee Andrew made a series of short phone calls, then a slightly longer one to someone he addressed as Giovanni, issuing what sounded like low-toned but precise instructions.

Moving between the two capitals as freely as he did, Andrew needed to do little else apart from summoning a taxi, apprising his housekeeper of the situation and locking up the villa.

Their cab had arrived and was drawn up outside the ornamental iron gates. When Andrew had helped Bel in, he gave the driver her address, instructing, 'Make it as quick as you can.'

The man nodded, and with a fine disregard for other road-users set off to cover the comparatively short distance in record time.

As soon as their driver's attention was on the road Bel turned to Andrew, a little frown marring her smooth forehead, and asked abruptly, 'How did you know where I was staying?'

Clearly his mind was on other things, and the question caught him unawares. He raised a dark brow. 'Staying?'

Knowing he was far from obtuse, she guessed he was playing for time. 'You gave the driver my address without asking me.'

His eyes narrowed and, watching him, she saw a flicker of something that might have been chagrin across his face. Then with a faint shrug he suggested, 'Perhaps you mentioned it yesterday.'

'I'm quite sure I haven't mentioned it,' she denied flatly.

'In that case I must have learnt it from your ex-fiancé,' he said smoothly.

No, she didn't believe a word. It was *possible* that Roderick had told him, but most improbable… Yet if he hadn't learnt it from Roderick, how had he known?

She was still mulling over the puzzle when they reached their destination.

Telling the driver they would be ten minutes or so, Andrew followed Bel up to the flat.

He waited in the living room while she changed into a lilac-coloured silk-jersey suit and smart shoes, coiled her pale blonde hair into a smooth chignon and quickly repacked.

When she came back he was standing, feet a little apart, hands in his pockets, looking out across the sunny square. Once again the back of his dark head stirred some memory in her mind, but before she could pinpoint it he turned to face her.

'All set?' Though he spoke casually, she sensed he was eager to be gone.

'I'd just like to phone my father and let him know I'm coming home. I haven't been in touch with him since I arrived, and if he's been trying to get hold of me…'

'Will you tell him you're getting married?'

She shook her head. 'There's such a lot to explain. I'd rather talk to him when I get back…' As she spoke she was dialling his office number.

It was answered at the second ring. 'Mr Grant's secretary speaking.'

'Hello, Joan, this is Bel. Can I speak to Dad?'

'Sorry, your father isn't in,' Joan Mitchell told her. 'He has a meeting with Mr Hargreaves at the bank, followed by a business lunch and an afternoon appointment. I'm not expecting him back much before three-thirty. Would you like him to call you, or can I give him a message?'

'Will you tell him I'm leaving Rome shortly, and I'll see him some time this evening?'

'Certainly. Oh, by the way, earlier today Mr Harmen was asking how long you'd be away.'

'Why? What did he want?' Bel asked without enthusiasm.

'Your last report on the Ridgeley account. I found it for him.' With uncharacteristic venom, Joan added, 'I can't help but *dislike* that man.'

'I'm not too fond of him myself,' replied Bel, then said sharply, 'Has he been bothering you?'

'Not in the way you mean. I just get the feeling he isn't to be trusted, either on a personal or a business basis.'

'I feel the same. Though it's probably pure prejudice. He has been with the firm a long time, and Dad trusts him… Oh, speaking of Dad, when you talk to him can you emphasise that there's absolutely nothing wrong, everything's fine.'

'Yes, I'll do that.'

'Thanks. Bye.'

As Bel replaced the receiver Andrew asked, 'Trouble at the office?'

'Not really. Just a mutual dislike and distrust of our company secretary...' In response to some faint stirring, some shadowy half-knowledge lurking on the periphery of her mind, she went on, 'His name's Mortimer Harmen...I suppose you don't know him?'

'No.' Andrew's denial was short and decisive. 'Ready to go?'

'I just have to return the key.'

While she had a quick word with the *custode di casa* Andrew carried her luggage down, and within minutes they were on their way to the airport.

During the journey, while Bel struggled to get her thoughts in order and catch up with events, Andrew listened to the taxi driver's long-winded account of the birth of his new son and heir with commendable patience.

He was a strange, complex man, Bel thought, hearing him offer congratulations. Tough and ruthless in some ways, and with layers of hardness that gave him the strength of laminated wood, yet he had a basic warmth, a genuine liking for people.

By the time they reached the airport all the formalities had been completed, and the plane was only waiting for its passengers to board before starting its flight to London.

Bel, who had never travelled in a privately owned plane before, was staggered by the quiet opulence of the executive jet.

As soon as the plane was airborne Andrew excused himself and disappeared into the cockpit while Bel was shown into a comfortable lounge by a steward with a thin face and a soft Irish brogue, who introduced himself as Patrick O'Brien.

When she was alone, having refused the champagne and caviar she'd been offered, Bel poured herself a glass of the iced water she'd requested and took a look around.

Outside the windows she could see a sky of clear forget-me-not-blue resting on a carpet of white cotton wool clouds.

Inside, a cushioned couch and two pale green velvet upholstered armchairs, with a low table between them, stood on a blue and gold Persian carpet.

Opposite a well-stocked bar was a video screen and music centre, and on the bulkhead, echoing the colours of the carpet, hung a glorious Venetian scene by Canaletto.

By way of contrast, on a small, businesslike desk lay a briefcase and a laptop computer.

At the far end of the cabin was a luxurious shower room and toilet and, to her surprise, a small, but sumptuous bedroom.

The sight of the lavish, silk-sheeted bed, and the mirror above it, made her go cold. Innocent as she was, she could imagine only one reason for it being there.

Yet why did she feel so shocked? It wasn't a boy she had agreed to marry, but an experienced man with a powerful libido. His amount of sexual expertise, not to mention his own admission, confirmed that he hadn't lived like a monk.

Though he *had* said he preferred to have one special woman, she tried to reassure herself. But, having seen this distasteful little set-up, could she believe him? He had been cavalier with the truth in other directions.

Apart from the fact that he was a superb lover, she knew little of the private man, and this bed—a bed that breathed seduction—seemed to provide a dark and disturbing insight into his character...

Did his ironic smile, his stunning charm, conceal murky depths? What if he was planning to take her hand and lead *her* to that erotic love-nest?

Alarmed and agitated, shaken to the core to realise just what kind of man she might have fallen in love with, she retreated hurriedly and took a seat in one of the armchairs.

She had barely settled herself when Andrew appeared, carrying a small black leather case which he placed on the table.

Taking off his light jacket, he tossed it aside, then, coming up behind her, put a hand beneath her chin and tilted her head back. As he bent to kiss her his other hand slid down to find the soft curves beneath her loose jacket.

Feeling sick, she caught his wrist and in mute protest held his hand away from her breast.

'Don't worry,' he murmured against her mouth. 'Patrick is very discreet. He won't come through without knocking.'

The painful knowledge that her suspicions had been correct made her jerk her head aside and demand bitterly, 'How many other women have you said that to when you were planning to seduce them?'

Bel felt rather than saw him stiffen.

'Do you imagine I usually mix business with pleasure?'

'Why else would you need a bed?'

'Apart from to sleep in, you mean?' His tone was

calm, even slightly amused, but she knew he was rattled.

'I've never heard of anyone *watching* themselves sleep,' she retorted contemptuously.

'So you think I'm a lech?' He was quietly, coldly *furious*.

Her hands were clenched into fists, the nails biting into her palms. 'What else *can* I think?'

He came to stand facing her, his jaw set, his eyes, icy as a winter sea, holding hers.

'I bought this plane some eighteen months ago, just as it stood. The only things I have added personally are the desk and the Canaletto. I have never made use of the bed, either for sleeping or for any other purpose. Most of my journeys have been short and purely business, and while *I've* owned the plane *you* are the only woman to have flown in it...'

The silence lengthened, the only sound the muffled roar of the engines, while relief ran through her like a warm tide.

'I hope you believe me?'

Mortified by her own stupid blunder, she stammered, 'Yes, I—I do believe you. I shouldn't have jumped to conclusions.'

'No, you shouldn't.' Though he spoke softly, the edge to his voice could have cut glass.

Flushing, she said helplessly, 'But I really don't know you very well, and that room—'

She broke off abruptly as a tap at the door announced the luncheon trolley.

His gaze releasing hers, Andrew moved to shield her confusion from the steward's glance, saying easily, 'Thank you, Patrick. We'll serve ourselves.'

When the man had gone, Andrew said evenly, some

of the hardness leaving his face, 'If the bedroom offends you, I'll have it stripped out.'

His attitude made it clear that as far as he was concerned the subject was now closed, and he added with a touch of wry humour, 'When we're married, should we decide to join the Mile-High Club, there's always the couch.'

'The Mile-High Club?'

'An élite few who are able to make love in a plane; that is to say more than a mile above the earth's surface.'

While she blushed rosily he turned his attention to the beautifully presented seafood platter and raised an enquiring brow.

At her nod, he helped her to a selection of smoked oysters, wafer-thin salmon, king prawns and watercress, accompanied by dainty triangles of brown bread and butter and a glass of perfectly chilled Pouilly-Fumé.

As the plane carried them through a cloudless blue sky Bel ate without speaking, her eyes on her plate while she struggled to regain her composure. If only she hadn't made such a mess of things...

After a while, a surreptitious glance from beneath her long, silky lashes showed that Andrew, who was pouring coffee from the heated jug, now wore a casual, relaxed air, as if he'd forgotten the uncomfortable little incident.

But, only too aware that she owed him an apology, Bel was unable to do the same. Accepting her cup, she met his eyes and said jerkily, 'It wasn't so much the bedroom that offended me as the thought of how it might have been used. But I had no right to...to...'

'As my fiancée, you had every right to ask for an explanation.'

'I only wish I *had* asked, rather than jumping to conclusions.' Her eyes filled with contrite tears. 'I'm sorry I said what I did.'

He lifted her hand and carried it to his lips. 'Don't cry, my darling. It's forgotten.'

My darling… Though she knew it meant nothing, after what had happened the endearment was a precious and unexpected gift that lightened her heart.

'And as my fiancée,' he went on, after a moment, 'it's high time you had a look at these.'

Reaching for the case he'd brought in earlier, he took a seat beside her and, flipping open the lid, displayed a selection of superb and unusual engagement rings.

Smiling at her stunned expression, he said, 'This time I thought *you* might like to choose.'

There was a ruby, a topaz, an aquamarine, a sapphire, a garnet, an amethyst and a glorious emerald that even Bel's untrained eye could see was in a class by itself.

When she merely stared at the dazzling array, he added, 'Of course, we can buy a ring in London if you don't see anything here that takes your fancy.'

'No, it's not that,' she managed. 'They're all gorgeous. I'm just…overwhelmed.'

'Then I suggest you take your time and try them to see which you like the best.'

Bel's fingers were long and slender, the well cared for nails pale shiny ovals. Lifting her left hand, he slipped the rings on one by one, giving her time to admire them.

She could almost have picked blindfolded. Each of them looked good in its own way, and they all fitted perfectly, but when he came to the last, however, the emerald slid onto her third finger as if made for it.

It was a huge stone in an antique setting, and it could have appeared overpowering, but on Bel's slim, yet strong hand it looked wonderful, and she caught her breath as the magnificent gem flashed green fire.

'Yours, I think?' Andrew asked simply.

Cheeks a little flushed, eyes shining, she nodded, and, now they were officially engaged, waited for him to kiss her.

When he made no move to do so, she said, 'Thank you. It's the most beautiful ring I've ever seen. It looks genuinely old.'

'It is. I asked Giovanni to send a selection so you could have a choice, but this particular ring was my maternal grandmother's. It was said to have belonged to one of the infamous Borgias, though I rather doubt it.'

'I wouldn't mind if it had.'

'And you're not superstitious about emeralds?'

'No.'

'That's good.' His voice deepening, roughening, he added, 'It matches your lovely eyes.'

Made breathless by the way he was looking at her, she swallowed hard and, knowing the ring must be worth a king's ransom, said huskily, 'You'd better put it safely away.'

'Leave it on.'

'But it must be very valuable. Suppose I lost it, or it was stolen…'

'It's insured,' he said calmly, 'and I see no point in keeping your engagement ring locked away in a safe. I want you to wear it to prove you're mine.'

Her flush deepening, her lips a little parted, she waited. Surely he'd kiss her now?

But he got up abruptly and after snapping the case shut, put it on the desk. When he turned to her his face was taut, the tanned skin stretched over the strong bone structure, a hard flush lying along his cheekbones.

His desire, held rigidly in check though it was, beat against her like the white-hot heat from a furnace, melting her very bones. She rose to her feet.

For once his intuition wasn't working, and he misread the signals. A muscle jumped in his jaw. 'There's no need to panic,' he told her caustically. 'Just because you're wearing my ring I have no intention of trying to drag you off to bed and seduce you.'

So, even though he'd said her scathing words had been forgotten, they had left a mark.

'I never thought you had,' she informed him, with a coolness she was far from feeling, and wondered if there was anything she could do to erase them from his memory.

When he made no move, she went to him and, putting her arms around his neck, asked provocatively, 'But aren't you at least going to kiss me?'

Tightly, he said, 'If I do I might not be able to keep my hands off you.'

Standing on tiptoe, she brushed her lips across his. 'Who said I wanted you to?'

With a kind of groan he pulled her against him. His mouth had just closed over hers when there was a tap at the door. With a muttered oath he released her and ~ved away.

~~hen Patrick O'Brien came in to remove the trolley ~~re standing several feet apart, the picture of decorum, though constraint stretched between them like invisible threads.

The steward cleared his throat. 'If you can spare a minute, sir, Captain Drummond would like a word with you.'

With a nod, Andrew followed the man out.

He was gone for what seemed an age, and Bel found herself wondering if he was staying away deliberately, to give them both time to cool down.

When he finally returned it was to inform her that they would be landing in about twenty minutes. Then, with distant politeness, he began to talk about their immediate plans.

'As soon as we get back to London I'll make the necessary arrangements for us to be married. A special licence—in other words permission to be married without the need for banns to be called—should enable the ceremony to take place in two or three days' time... I presume that in the circumstances you have no objection to a small, quiet wedding?'

Thrown by his aloof manner, the formal way he was consulting her, she pulled herself together and said quietly, 'No.'

'I thought St Giles's Church, Shoreland Square. The vicar there is a friend of mine... Unless you have any other preference?'

'No,' she said again.

Then, recalling what in-depth and prolonged discussions had taken place between herself and Roderick on the same subject, she thought with a kind of wry amusement that this time she and her fiancé could have been discussing what kind of filling she fancied in her sandwich.

Except that that might have taken more deciding.

But somehow, with Andrew, the wedding and where it was to take place seemed relatively unimportant. What was important was the man himself. Their marriage. Their future together.

If only he loved her... She shook herself mentally. It was no use repining. He wanted her, and for the moment at least that would have to be enough.

But would it be enough? Suppose he got tired of her? She had always wanted to have a marriage that would last, to fall in love with a man who would return her love and give her a lifetime's commitment, especially if there were to be children.

However, fate, it seemed, had made the choice for her, and, though gambling on a one-sided love like this surely had to be a kind of insanity, there was no going back.

And perhaps if she did her best, gave him all she had to give, her own love might strike an answering spark...?

All at once she became aware that Andrew was watching her, waiting for an answer to a question she hadn't even heard. 'I—I'm sorry?'

'I asked if you will be having any bridesmaids?'

She shook her head. 'It would be awkward. The ones I intended to have all knew and liked Roderick. And if I'm just wearing a suit...'

'But you won't be just wearing a suit.' His voice was adamant. 'Even though the wedding party will be small, I want a traditional bride with a white dress and a veil.'

Face half averted, looking down at her hands clasped together in her lap, Bel agreed, 'Very well.'

His eyes admiring the pure line of her profile, the curve of lashes that almost brushed her cheek, he asked crisply, 'Is there anyone, apart from your immediate family, that you'd care to invite?'

'I'd like Dad to be there, of course, and Ellen, if she's home. But no one else, really. What about you?'

Andrew's jaw tightened. 'My mother and stepfather are both dead, killed in a hotel fire.' Surprising her, he went on, 'I've a stepbrother, Jonathan, I'll ask to be my best man. But there's no one else apart from Jonathan's wife, Penny. Perhaps she could act as your matron of honour?' Then he added abruptly, 'Will your father give you away?'

'I hope so. Though of course he won't be expecting...I mean, the whole thing will come as a surprise to him.' *Not to say shock.*

'Incidentally, what have you told him so far?'

'Only that my engagement to Roderick is over.'

'What was his reaction?' he asked, then added with a slight edge, 'I understand he thinks the world of you?'

On the surface both questions seemed innocent enough, but, sensing disturbing undercurrents, Bel answered only the first. 'As you might expect, he was staggered and, I think, upset. He liked Roderick and thought we were well suited.'

'But he didn't attempt to change your mind?'

'No.' Stiffly, she added, 'If he had, in the circumstances it would have been useless.'

'Did you tell him the circumstances?'

Shaking her head, she said with a tinge of bitterness, 'I was hardly proud of them.'

'So he knows nothing about me?'

'No. I'll have to explain things this evening. I don't know how he'll feel about it.'

But she did know. He would be convinced that

taken leave of her senses when he discovered that within three days of her engagement ending she was planning to marry a virtual stranger.

Picking up her anxiety, Andrew frowned. 'Perhaps I should come with you?'

'I think it would be better if I went alone. I'd like to give him time to get used to the idea before he meets you.'

'Very well.' He regarded her thoughtfully. 'The flat you rent—is it a furnished one?'

'Yes.'

'So it won't take you too long to clear it?'

'You mean after we're married?'

'I mean today. I want you to move in with me.'

'Oh, but I—'

'Don't worry, there are several guest rooms. I won't ask you to share my bed until we're man and wife.'

'It isn't that,' she admitted honestly. 'I just hadn't got round to thinking about moving.'

'What is there to think about? Surely all you have to do is pack your personal possessions and hand in the key?'

'Yes, I suppose so.'

'Then why not get it done? You'll need the remaining time to buy your wedding dress and shop for a trousseau.'

Before she could form any further protest, he added, 'I'll drop you off there. Leave the luggage you've got with you in the car. I'll give you a couple of hours, then send Bridges round to collect the rest of your things. What time do you intend to go to your father's?'

'As soon as he's home from the office.'

'Do you want Bridges to take you?'

She shook her head. 'I'll use my own car.'

'Very well. I'll expect you for dinner…shall we say seven-thirty? I have the penthouse apartment in the Lambeck Building.'

Once again his choice of a home surprised her. The Lambeck Building was quiet and select and unobtrusive, a haven for wealthy aristocrats rather than the *nouveau riche*.

'There's an underground car park and my bay is number three on the left, next to the lifts. Tell Bancroft, the security guard, that I told you to come straight up.'

Bel drew a swift, shaky breath. Until three days ago she had thought of herself as a modern young woman with a mind of her own, capable of making her own decisions and running her own affairs.

Nothing in her experience had prepared her for a man of Andrew's calibre, for the way he had blown into her life like a whirlwind and taken her over.

The weather was still holding good, the sky clear and bright, when, some five minutes later, they made a perfect landing and taxied towards the airport buildings to get the formalities over.

Bridges, grey-haired and sedate, was waiting for them with a gleaming limousine, and by mid-afternoon they were drawing up outside the black spiky railings of number ten Clorres Place.

Andrew accompanied Bel down the steps and waited until she'd found the key. 'Seven-thirty,' he reminded her, and after dropping a quick kiss on her lips departed.

Closing the door, she felt a sudden and keen sense of loss… It just proved how bad she'd got it, she told herself with an attempt at humour.

But really it wasn't funny. In such a short time he'd become the centre of her universe, the sun around which her whole being revolved. If he ever got tired of her, and left her, the rest of her life would be spent in shadow...

Oh, come on! She was behaving like some foolish, half-hysterical heroine in a cheap novelette, rather than an independent woman with plenty of common sense.

If this was what love did to you, she thought wryly, she'd have been better off not tangling with it. Except she'd had no choice.

Putting her ring carefully on one side, she dug a spare suitcase and some boxes out of the glory-hole and started on the task of sorting out and bidding farewell to her former life.

Clad in old, too-tight jeans and a shrunken T-shirt, with a scarf tied turban-fashion over her hair, Bel cleaned through the flat and assembled what she wanted to take, leaving on one side a change of clothing for when she'd finished.

By the time Bridges knocked she was all packed, and several plastic bin-liners containing clothing and items for the nearest charity shop were tied up and waiting.

A streak of dust across her cheek, her turban slipping drunkenly over one ear, she opened the door.

Blue-grey eyes travelled over her and did a double take before they lit with laughter.

Flustered, not only by Andrew's unconcealed amusement but by the realisation that he was now wearing a smart business suit, and only too conscious of the hip-hugging jeans and the way the T-shirt flattened her breasts and rode up to show an inch or so of naked flesh, she said crossly, 'I thought you were sending Bridges.'

'It's just as well I didn't...'

Following her in, Andrew drew her close, his cheek against hers and his hands, discovering she was wearing nothing beneath the T-shirt, moving to follow the elegant length of her bare spine.

'You're so incredibly sexy in that charlady's get-up, it might have made him dissatisfied with his new lady-friend...'

Heart racing, the blood starting to pound in her ears, Bel pulled herself free and stepped back, unwinding the turban. 'How do you know he's got a new lady-friend?' Even in her own ears her voice sounded squeaky.

Andrew gave a little grimace, but allowed her to call the tune. 'He asked for a couple of hours off "around teatime", explaining that he'd "made arrangements" before he knew I'd be returning. I winkled the rest out of him, and, never one to stand in the way of true love—' Andrew's smile was sardonic '—told him to take the rest of the day off.'

Bel bit her lip.

Then, realising that Andrew had noted her reaction, she threw up a smokescreen. 'Oh, well, I suppose everything can stay where it is. The rent's paid until the end of the month, so there's no particular hurry.'

He shook his head. 'I've every intention of dealing with it now.' While she hovered uneasily by the open door Andrew began to carry the various boxes out to his Jaguar.

'Don't bother with the charity bags,' she told him. 'The shop will be closed by now.'

But, gathering them up, he said, 'I'll put them in the boot. Bridges can take them tomorrow.'

When the place was finally clear, Andrew queried, 'All done?'

'Yes. As soon as I've showered and changed, I'm off to see Dad.'

'And you wouldn't like me to come with you?'

Not looking forward to trying to explain the situation—a situation she herself still felt was incredible—Bel thought of having him there to lean on, and wavered.

But would it be for the best? Andrew's presence could prove to be a two-edged sword. It might be easier to speak to her father frankly, to give her reasons and reassure him, if they were alone.

'No, I don't think so.'

'Sure?'

'Quite sure.'

About to turn away, he paused to inform her almost casually, 'Though there are still one or two loose ends to tie up, a special licence should be through by Thursday. The Reverend John Blackthorn will be happy to perform the ceremony. He tells me that a marriage can take place in church between eight a.m. and six p.m., but as there are already two weddings booked for the afternoon he's asked that we make ours a morning one. Ten-thirty, if that suits you?'

Hoping she didn't sound as dazed as she felt, Bel agreed, 'Yes, of course.'

'Then I'll finalise all the arrangements.'

At the door, he took her face between his hands and looked at her searchingly, 'You're very close to your father, aren't you?' When she half nodded, he said with sudden urgency, 'You won't let him talk you out of it?'

All he'd shown her so far had been his strength. Now all at once he was human, vulnerable, with a chink in the armour of his certainty.

She felt a rush of tenderness. 'No. I won't let him talk me out of it. I doubt if he'll even try to. All he's ever wanted is my happiness.'

Some strong emotion she was unable to identify flickered across Andrew's face and was gone. Bending his dark head, he kissed her, a brief, hard kiss, searing in its intensity. A moment later he was taking the steps two at a time.

A hand to her mouth, Bel stood where she was until the sleek car had drawn away. Then, squaring her shoulders, she went in to shower and change for what she guessed would prove to be one of the most difficult meetings of her life.

CHAPTER SEVEN

As Bel let herself into the big Regency house on Dunbarton Street her father appeared in the hall.

She went to him and kissed his cheek. 'I tried to ring you when I got to Rome, but your phone was playing up.'

'I know; I had it fixed. Is everything all right?' He looked hopeful rather than anxious, she noted.

'Yes, everything's fine.' She managed to sound more confident than she felt.

Peter Grant beamed. 'I guessed it was nothing but a storm in a teacup. Though you're usually very level-headed, when someone's in love little things can get blown up out of all proportion.'

Suddenly realising what he was getting at, Bel began to shake her head, but he was going on.

'Isn't Roderick with you? I thought he might—'

'Dad,' she broke in urgently, 'you've got it all wrong. Roderick and I haven't made it up.'

'You haven't? Then why have you come home so soon? I felt sure he must have been in touch and—'

'No, it's nothing like that. Look, let's go and sit down. It's a long story.'

Looking worried now, Peter Grant followed his daughter through to the handsome living room, which faced west and overlooked the well-kept garden.

The room was light and airy, its French windows

open to the early-evening breeze. A low sun shining through the branches of a beech tree decorated the striped wallpaper with a moving pattern of leaves.

As Bel took a seat her father said, 'Before we start, if you're thinking of staying for dinner I'd better let Mrs Piggot know.'

'No, I won't be staying.'

'A sherry, then?'

'Better not. I'm driving.'

Taking the armchair opposite, Peter Grant studied his daughter for a moment, then remarked, 'Somehow you look different.'

Amazed at his perspicacity, Bel said, 'I *am* different. Since I saw you last my whole life's changed. I know that sounds a bit over the top—' she tried to smile '—but there's no other way of putting it.'

Sensing the real anxiety behind her attempted lightness, he said, 'You'd better tell me about it.'

Her ash-blonde hair was loose, and the breeze flicked a silky strand across her cheek. Pushing it back, she jumped in at the deep end. 'When I got engaged to Roderick I thought I loved him…but now I've fallen in love, *really* in love, with another man. It makes what I felt for Roderick seem no more than mere fondness.'

'Ah…and it was because of this other man that your engagement ended?'

She flushed. 'Well, yes…in a way.'

In some respects it would have been a relief to make a clean breast of it and tell her father the whole truth. But, having thought about it, she knew it was better not to. It would only upset him, and it wouldn't reflect too well on Andrew.

The two men were the people in her life that she cared for most, and it was desperately important to her that when they did meet they hit it off and liked each other.

'So who is he?' Peter pursued. 'How long have you known him?'

'His name's Andrew Storm. I—I haven't really known him very long... I suppose you could say it was love at first sight, though that probably sounds rather silly to you.'

But her father was shaking his head. 'That's how it was when I met your mother. I fell in love with her the moment I saw her.' His face grew soft. 'Later she told me she'd felt the same way about me.'

Then briskly, as though half ashamed of showing his emotion, he said, 'So tell me about this Andrew Storm. How old is he?'

'In his early thirties. He's a banker and a business-man.'

'Successful?'

'Very. He has worldwide business interests.'

'Can't say I've ever heard of him. He must keep a low profile.'

'I imagine he does. In some ways he's a very...' She hesitated. 'A very private person—a man who likes to play his cards close to his chest.'

Picking up the slight strain in his daughter's manner, Peter asked sharply, 'He's not married?'

She shook her head. 'No, he's single.'

His relief that she wasn't entangled with a married man patent, her father asked, 'What's he like?'

'Sophisticated, assured. A powerful, intelligent, charismatic man with a sharp, clear mind.'

'Arrogant?'

'He has strong views on most things without being opinionated,' she answered truthfully.

'I meant arrogant when it comes to women.'

'Just confident,' she said, slightly less truthfully. 'But he's far from insensitive and he has a kind of infectious *joie de vivre*.'

'Where did you first meet him?'

Bel said carefully, 'I bumped into him in a restaurant one lunchtime, then I met him again at the Bentincks'.'

'So he's a friend of Roderick's?'

'A business acquaintance.'

'What's he like to look at?'

'Stunningly attractive, yet I've seen no sign of personal vanity...'

As she paused, struggling to find the right words to describe a man like Andrew, Peter caught the ball and ran with it. 'Short?'

'Tall. Over six feet.'

'Fair?'

'Dark.'

'And no doubt incredibly handsome,' Peter teased.

'Yes, but not in a film star-ish way. His face is too strong. He has a hawk's profile and a squarish chin, and he's built like Superman...'

'Go on.'

Bel's face softened and glowed. 'He has eyes the colour of woodsmoke, a mouth that can look either warm or austere, and his voice is spellbinding...'

Her father chuckled. 'My, you have got it badly.'

Laughing and blushing, she admitted, 'You could say that.'

Studying her, he observed, 'You look like a sixteen-year-old in love for the very first time.'

'Whereas I'm a twenty-three-year-old in love for the very first time.'

With sudden seriousness, he said, 'I just don't want you to get hurt.'

'I'll try not to,' Bel promised lightly.

She was gathering herself, wondering how to break the news of the forthcoming wedding, when her father observed, 'You've told me everything about this man you love except the most important thing. How does he feel? Does he love you?'

Ignoring the stab of pain that lanced through her, Bel smiled brilliantly. 'He wants to marry me. In fact we're already engaged.' Holding out the hand she'd kept hidden in her lap, she displayed her ring.

Peter whistled. 'A fast worker, and judging by the size of that emerald he's got more than enough to keep the wolf from the door.'

'I'd marry him if I had to buy a catapult to do that,' she said dryly. 'The only thing I'm sorry about is the *way* it happened. I never wanted to hurt Roderick or his parents…'

But Peter was frowning, a puzzled expression on his nice-looking face. 'If you didn't break it off with Roderick until Saturday…and it's only Monday now, how on earth have you managed to get engaged and buy a ring?'

Bel took a deep breath. 'I know it seems incredible…I can hardly believe it myself. But Andrew's got his own private jet and he followed me to Rome. The ring is a family heirloom; it belonged to his Italian grandmother—'

Frowning, Peter broke in, 'Surely he can't be Italian with a name like Andrew Storm?'

'His mother was Italian and his father was English. He was born and brought up in England but he speaks Italian fluently.' She glanced down at the emerald. 'He gave me this on the flight back to England. I was a bit worried about it being so valuable, but he said he wanted me to wear it.'

There was a thoughtful silence, then Peter said slowly, 'No one can blame you for breaking your first engagement when you realised it had been a mistake, but don't you think it would be best to keep the second quiet for a while, give things a chance to blow over?'

'Well, I—'

'If you don't, it might make Roderick look a fool, and people are bound to think you've been caught on the rebound. Perhaps if you waited a month or two—'

'Dad,' she broke in desperately, 'please listen. Neither Andrew nor I want to wait.'

Peter shook his head. 'It doesn't do to rush into things. Why not give yourself time, and if you still feel the same announce your engagement at Christmas? Then perhaps a spring wedding—'

'We've decided to get married as soon as possible. That's why we flew back today.'

She saw the shock hit him like a punch on the jaw.

For a full minute neither spoke, and the silence seemed to hold its breath. Then, sounding confused, he asked, 'But why such haste?'

He was a decent and good man, with values to match, and, knowing she couldn't tell him the truth, she said as lightly as possible, 'We want to be together, and neither of us can see any real reason to wait. Andrew's getting a special licence and we're hoping to be married on Thursday morning at ten-thirty.'

'At the register office?'

'No, St Giles's Church.'

Arrested by the look on her father's face, she was about to ask if anything was the matter when he said quietly, 'I'm glad you chose St Giles's. That's the church your mother and I were married at.'

Getting to his feet hastily, he turned to stare through the window, evincing a keen interest in a blackbird that was splashing about in the shallow stone bird-bath.

Her eyes misty, Bel was pleased to be able to tell him, 'It was Andrew's suggestion. I gather he knows the vicar there.'

Then she went on a little awkwardly, 'Though it will obviously be a very quiet wedding, with just Andrew's stepbrother as best man and his wife as matron of honour, he wants me to have a long dress and a veil.'

Her father turned to smile at her. 'All the trimmings, eh? Good for him. I wouldn't want it to seem like some rushed, hole-and-corner affair.'

Greatly relieved, she asked, 'Dad…you will give me away?'

'I'll be proud to. You'll come back here for a small reception, won't you? Mrs Piggot will jump at the chance to use her talents and put on a buffet… And as the bride's father it will be my privilege to buy your wedding finery and a knock-your-eye-out trousseau.'

Bursting into tears, Bel jumped up and, throwing her arms around his neck, hugged him.

When he'd patted her back, he fished in his pocket and, producing a neatly folded handkerchief, said mildly, 'Perhaps you'd better make haste and mop up. Any second now Mrs Piggot will be in to tell me dinner's ready…and you know how she loves a good soap opera,' he added dryly.

'Doesn't she just?' Bel grinned as she obediently wiped her eyes and blew her nose. 'And, speaking of dinner, I ought to be on my way. Andrew's expecting me at seven-thirty.'

'You're eating at his place?'

'I'm staying there,' she admitted, adding truthfully, 'He said he'd be happy for me to have one of the guest rooms.' As her father followed her into the hall she explained, 'Because there's so little time, and a great deal to do, before I came here I cleared my flat and handed in the key.'

Peter's brows drew together in a frown. 'If you've plumped for the traditional scene, on the wedding morning the bride and groom shouldn't see each other until they get to church.'

'I hadn't really thought that far ahead,' she admitted.

'And the bride should travel to church with the person who's giving her away.' With a touch of humour, he added, 'You're my only daughter and I don't want to miss out on the excitement.'

She gave him a hug. 'Then what if I bring all my finery and sleep here Wednesday night?'

Seriously, he asked, 'Would that cause any problems?'

'Of course not. It's the ideal solution.'

'Marvellous!' He beamed his pleasure.

Sounding dazed, she said, 'I can hardly believe I'm getting married in just three days' time.'

'Thinking about it,' her father remarked, 'I suppose I shall have to start looking for a new European marketing director?'

'Things have happened so quickly that we've had no time to discuss it, but Andrew did once say that he would prefer his wife not to work, to be free to travel with him…he's a person who values companionship.'

Surprising her, Peter said, 'That's the nicest thing you've said about him. I've often wished I'd spent more time with your mother while I had the chance, instead of making work my god.'

Then, shrugging off past regrets, he said, 'So when do I get to meet this man of yours?'

She smiled. 'As soon as possible. Come over tonight, if you like.'

He shook his head. 'I've promised to play bowls, and it's too late to drop out now.'

'What about dinner tomorrow night?'

'Fine.'

At the door, she said, 'I'll ring you to make the final arrangements. If you should happen to want me, Andrew has the penthouse apartment in the Lambeck Building on Park Lane. I'm afraid I don't know the phone number off hand.'

She had kissed his cheek and was about to turn away when a thought stopped her in her tracks. 'I've been so taken up with telling you my news, I almost forgot to ask if you've heard from Ellen?'

'No.'

Bel gave an exasperated sigh. 'She rang me just as I was about to set off for Rome. She *promised* she'd call you.'

'Did you mention the shares?'

'No, there wasn't time.'

'I haven't been able to contact her, so I take it she wasn't at home?'

'No.'

'Oh, well, she can't be talked into doing anything stupid while she's still in Paris... Did she tell you where she was staying?'

'Hotel Colbert. Apparently it's close to the Champs-Élysées.'

'I'll give her a ring straight away, just to be on the

safe side... Oh, and Bel, don't worry about Roderick and what can't be altered. You've found the man you really love, so be happy.'

Limp with reaction, but only too delighted that her father had taken it so well, Bel drove through the early-evening traffic to Park Lane.

When she reached the Lambeck Building's car park and stopped at the barrier, a well-built, good-looking young man wearing a blue uniform appeared in the doorway of the glass booth. Bancroft, presumably.

Before she could give him Andrew's message, he queried politely, 'Miss Grant? Mr Storm asked me to let him know the minute you arrived. Please go straight up.'

The barrier was promptly raised.

With a nod of thanks she drove through and, smiling ironically at the contrast, parked her six-year-old white Cavalier in bay three between the limousine and the Jaguar.

As she turned towards the lifts the doors of the nearest opened and Andrew appeared.

Just the sight of him made her heart pick up speed and sent shivers of excitement running through her.

To cover her confusion, she remarked admiringly, 'I see Bancroft is efficient, as well as handsome.'

Andrew took her arm and led her into the lift. As the doors closed behind them he backed her against the wall and, pinning her there, demanded with mock menace, 'Are you trying to make me jealous?'

Looking up at him, she asked a shade breathlessly, 'Am I succeeding?'

'You'd better believe it.' He bent his head to kiss

her. It was a long, deep, achingly sweet kiss, that only ended when the lift stopped and the doors slid open.

In something of a daze, Bel found herself being escorted across a marble-floored foyer and into a spacious lounge that, though beautifully furnished, gave an impression of homely comfort rather than cool elegance.

There was an Adam fireplace, now full of flowers, several overflowing bookcases and floor-length windows which gave on to a long paved terrace that looked across Hyde Park. But, conscious only of the man by her side, Bel scarcely took it in.

'The kitchen and the dining room are on the left, and beyond that there's the tradesmen's entrance and the servants' quarters; the bedrooms are this way.'

He led her through double doors into a wide corridor with skylight windows and gleaming floors. Unusually, none of the floors was carpeted, all were of beautifully polished parquet, with simple off-white knotted wool rugs.

She noticed her suitcases were waiting, piled next to a Chippendale table that held a glorious display of mixed gladioli reflected in an oval gilt-framed wall mirror.

'My housekeeper's on holiday, so I'm afraid you'll have to do your own unpacking… The guest rooms are this side—' he threw open a series of doors '—take your pick. This is the master bedroom.'

Advancing into the light, ivory-walled room, whose long windows also led onto the terrace, Bel gazed across the park for a moment before turning to face him. 'I prefer this one.'

'Would you like me to move out until after the wedding?'

'*Would* you?'

'If you asked me to.'

Looking at him from beneath long, silky lashes, she said softly, 'I might just want you to stay.'

'Are you asking?'

'I'm asking.'

'I love a woman who knows her own mind.'

Pulling her into his arms, Andrew tilted her face up to his and, having kissed her deeply, queried, 'Hungry?'

Turning her face into his tanned throat, she murmured, 'For what?'

He said, as he'd said once before, 'I can provide whatever you need. Food, or...'

She lifted her head and met his smoky eyes steadily. 'Isn't it a bit early for dinner?'

Her words lit a flare of sensuality, Andrew's reaction prompting her to respond in a way that a few days before she wouldn't have believed possible.

While their mouths clung they began to undress each other. There was nothing leisurely in their actions; neither, it seemed, could wait to cast aside the barrier of clothes.

He stripped off her skirt and blouse and undies with deft ease while, having unfastened his shirt and tie, her inexperienced fingers fumbled and failed to undo the clip of his trousers.

Drawing back a little, she muttered, 'I'm not very good at this.'

While he helped her, he bit her earlobe. 'Last night you were so inhibited you wouldn't even have tried.'

'I wasn't inhibited,' she denied, remembering her own passionate response to his lovemaking. 'But it was the first time and—' She broke off in confusion.

'Were you disappointed?'

'No, of course not. It was *wonderful*.'

'The second time will be better.'

Incredibly, heart-stoppingly, it was.

Nothing in her experience had prepared her for the explosion of feeling that erupted when, lying on the big bed, they came together.

There was no long, slow seduction, no gradual build-up, but a fierce, driving need that demanded and took yet at the same time gave all and more than she could ever have asked.

Afterwards, as she lay in his arms, he kissed her with a gentle warmth that might have been mistaken for tenderness, and at that instant any lingering doubts that she was doing the right thing in marrying him faded and died.

It was some time before Andrew broke the contented silence to ask, 'How did the meeting with your father go?'

'Better than I'd dared hoped.'

As the fingers of his free hand began to roam, tracing her flat stomach and navel, the creamy skin of her hip and thigh, she gave him an edited version of the conversation.

'Of course it was a shock to him, but he's pleased we're getting married in church, and more than happy to give me away. He's going to arrange a small wedding reception at Dunbarton Street...'

Distracted by what Andrew was doing to her, she ended more than a shade breathlessly, 'He asked when you two were going to meet and I suggested dinner tomorrow night. I hope that's all right?'

'Mmm...' Andrew's assent was muffled, his mouth engaged in exploring the curve of her breast, his lips and tongue relearning the taste and texture of the pink nipple.

This time, having eliminated the need for urgency, his lovemaking was drawn out and leisurely. He made an erotic journey to discover and exploit every erogenous zone, finding his own pleasure in pleasuring her while he aroused an appetite she had thought was sated.

Not until she was on the point of begging did he move over her and with long, slow thrusts transport them both to a shared state of bliss.

When their heart-rate and breathing had returned to normal, he lifted himself away and, pulling on a short robe, disappeared through the door, returning after a minute or so with two glasses of chilled fruit juice.

He sat on the edge of the bed while they both drank thirstily, then, taking Bel's empty glass, said, 'Dinner will be about twenty minutes, if you want to shower first.'

As she went to find her belongings she heard the shower in one of the guest bathrooms running. Recalling Andrew's remark about liking to shower *à deux*, she was momentarily tempted to open the door and join him. But, remembering his mocking, 'I suppose we should save *some* excitement for when we're married', she resisted the temptation.

The bathroom adjoining the master bedroom was jade-green and sumptuous, large enough to hold a round walk-in bath and Jacuzzi as well as a normal-sized bath and shower.

When she had showered and dressed, Bel made her way to the stylish, L-shaped kitchen, where the table had been set for two and an open bottle of red wine left to breathe.

Andrew, a teatowel knotted around his lean hips,

was stirring a pan while he kept an eye on a couple of grilling pork steaks. To one side, in a glass bowl, was a freshly tossed green salad.

'When did you learn to cook?'

'While I was globe-trotting. It was a case of needs must...'

Bel sniffed appreciatively. 'Something smells delicious.'

'It's Pizzaiola sauce.'

'What does it have in it?'

'Fresh tomatoes, olive oil and garlic.'

'Is that all?'

He slanted her a teasing glance. 'Come and give me a kiss and I'll tell you the secret ingredient.'

She was about to obey when the phone rang.

'Who the devil can that be?' Andrew muttered.

'It might be Dad... I'll see, shall I?'

Before she could speak, a man's voice that definitely wasn't her father's said, 'I've just discovered there's been a slip-up...'

Silently, Bel held out the receiver.

'Yes?' Andrew said curtly, and then hearing the caller speak looked rattled just for a second, before a shutter came down. 'Yes... You'd better tell me...'

Bel frowned a little. Though she was unable to place it, the voice on the other end of the line had sounded oddly familiar.

'Very well, I'll deal with it... No, it shouldn't present any real problem...'

Having replaced the receiver, Andrew tested the sizzling meat and queried, 'Let's see, where were we? Ah, yes, you were about to come and give me a kiss.'

She had hoped he would casually mention who had

been on the phone, but clearly he wasn't going to, and she could hardly ask.

Telling herself firmly that it was none of her business, she went over and, standing on tiptoe, touched her lips to his tanned cheek.

'Call that a kiss?' he mocked. 'I can see I'm going to have to give you some lessons in the art of kissing.'

'I'll do my best to be an apt pupil,' she assured him.

'I'm sure you will be.' With a gleam in his eye, he added, 'You've shown a natural talent in other, not unrelated fields.'

It served her right for entering the fray, Bel thought as she watched him carry the food to the table. When it came to a battle of wits and words he could run rings round her.

With his customary politeness, he pulled out a chair for her and, having served her with pork and salad, proceeded to fill both long-stemmed glasses with Nuits-St-Georges.

She helped herself to some sauce, and, finding it was cordon bleu standard, said so. 'But you still haven't told me the secret ingredient,' she added.

He grinned briefly. 'I'll make that the prize for learning your lessons well.'

While they ate he told her something of his post-college travels, answering Bel's interested questions and describing the various far-flung countries he'd lived and worked in.

Afterwards they took their coffee into the lounge and sat side by side on the couch while they listened to Rodrigo's 'Guitar Concerto'.

When the lovely haunting music came to an end, Andrew stroked her cheek with a long, lean finger and said softly, 'You've been trying not to yawn for the past ten minutes, so I think an early night might be called for.'

He turned her face to his and kissed the tip of her nose. 'You'll have a busy day tomorrow, shopping for your wedding dress and trousseau... Incidentally, where were you intending to go?'

'I haven't had time to give it much thought... Harrods, probably.'

'You can charge whatever you get to my account.'

'Dad said *he* wanted to buy my dress and trousseau.'

Andrew's handsome face hardened. 'I'm more than happy to take care of my wife's needs.'

'But I'm *not* your wife yet,' she pointed out. 'And it's a father's privilege to pay for his daughter's wedding if he wants to.'

'Very well,' Andrew said coldly.

Touching his hand, Bel begged, 'Please don't be angry. I can't bear to hurt Dad's feelings...' Then she went on, perplexed, 'And to be honest, I fail to see what the problem is.'

There was a moment's silence, then with a little smile twisting his chiselled lips, Andrew admitted with wry self-mockery, 'Maybe I feel the need to maintain a psychological advantage.'

Genuinely puzzled, she said, 'I don't understand why.'

'Perhaps because I know you love *him* and you don't love *me*.'

'Do you *want* me to love you?' She held her breath.

'Oh, yes...' Something about the quietly spoken words made a chill run through her, and she shivered. The chill intensified as he went on, 'I want to be master of your heart as well as your body.'

She'd known from the start that he was fiercely possessive, so why did that simple declaration make her so uneasy?

Shaking her head, she said as steadily as possible, 'I've always considered that one-sided loving unbalances a relationship. It has to be more dangerous than a complete absence of love.'

With a strange, harsh note in his voice, he admitted, 'You could well be right.'

She swallowed hard. 'So in the circumstances it's just as well I *don't* love you.'

Desperate to change the subject, when he said nothing she harked back to ask, 'So what will you be doing tomorrow while I'm out choosing my finery?' And found herself hoping against hope that he might elect to come with her.

But, his manner casual now, as though the previous, fraught little conversation had never taken place, he told her, 'I've some business to take care of.'

'Oh… Well, perhaps we could have lunch together?' she queried hopefully. Then cursed herself. Having just denied that she loved him, it was stupid to demonstrate so plainly how besotted she really was.

But, as though he was unable to see it, Andrew said coolly, 'I'm afraid I won't be available for lunch. And surely if you're shopping at Harrods, it would make sense to eat there?'

Trying to hide her disappointment, Bel agreed, 'Of course it would. I wasn't thinking.' She made a great show of stifling a yawn. 'And you're right about my needing an early night.'

As though proffering an olive branch, he suggested, 'Before we turn in, perhaps you'd like to ring your father and finalise the dinner arrangements.'

'What shall I tell him?'

'Ask him to meet us at Morro Marengo…say, seven-thirty.'

'Morro Marengo?' Being the newest and most exclusive restaurant in town, it was notoriously difficult to get a table there.

'Luis Morro is a friend of mine,' Andrew informed her dryly. 'It was my bank that financed the venture.'

Equally dryly, she said, 'I should have guessed,' and picked up the phone.

If her father was surprised by the choice of venue, he gave no sign of it, saying merely, 'Fine, I'll be there.'

'How did the bowling go?'

'It was a disaster,' he admitted cheerfully. 'Pity I didn't drop out.'

'Did you manage to get hold of Ellen?' Bel asked.

'No, she's not at the Colbert any longer. She paid her bill and left early Saturday evening. Though she still doesn't seem to be home yet.'

'Oh, well, she's bound to…' Bel broke off. 'Wait a minute, I've just remembered something she said when she rang me… My taxi driver was banging on the door so I was only half listening, but she was talking about some gorgeous Frenchman named Jean-Claude who had invited her to his villa at Épernay…'

Peter groaned. 'Do you think she's been fool enough to go with him?'

'Well, even if she has, she'll come home sooner or later.' Bel tried to sound sanguine. 'And when she does surely you'll be able to talk to her before anyone else gets a chance?'

'I suppose so,' Peter agreed. 'It's just that things have gone strangely quiet—almost as if whoever's behind this knows damn well he's won and is simply biding his time.'

'Surely that's not possible?'

'It isn't possible for him to have a *controlling* interest. While you and I and Ellen hold onto our shares we have fifty-one per cent of the total.'

'Well, as you said earlier, she can't be talked into doing anything stupid while she's still in France, so quit worrying,' Bel said crisply.

Her father laughed. 'You're absolutely right, of course. There's no point in getting edgy. See you at seven-thirty tomorrow, then... Bye for now.' She was just about to replace the phone when he added, 'I'm looking forward to meeting my future son-in-law.'

When Bel relayed his rider to Andrew, he said evenly, 'Believe me, *I'm* looking forward to meeting my future father-in-law.'

The words themselves were mundane enough, but surely there was a shade, a nuance, of something not so innocuous?

Oh, don't be a fool! Bel told herself impatiently. Unlike most men, Andrew's reactions were rarely simple or straightforward. His smile, his voice, often held a touch of irony.

But this seemed to be something different, something darker, almost threatening...

Having watched her face for a moment, he began to kiss and nuzzle the side of her neck, sending her uneasy thoughts flying.

When she shivered in response, he murmured, 'I'm also looking forward to the first of our lessons, but I propose it takes place in bed.'

'Yes, Teacher.'

He rose and, taking her hands, pulled her to her feet. 'You go ahead. I've one quick call to make first.'

By the time he joined her in the big, luxurious bed she was comfortably drowsy, despite the promise of delight, and almost ready to slip into sleep.

Brushing a strand of silky hair away from her flushed face, he kissed her mouth and asked gently, 'Tired?'

'Yes.' Turning into his arms, she whispered, 'But not too tired.'

CHAPTER EIGHT

BY SIX O'CLOCK the following evening Bel was weary, but reasonably satisfied with her day's shopping. After trying on and rejecting more than a dozen wedding gowns she had finally found one that was all she could have hoped for.

Made of ivory silk, with a fitted bodice and full skirt, it relied on the beautiful medieval style for its romantic impact. Plain silk slippers and a filmy veil on a narrow diadem completed the picture.

Her excitement rising, she had also bought a black chiffon dress to wear that evening, and a mink-coloured silk suit with tangerine accessories.

There had been no mention of a honeymoon, but after the wedding she would need something to change into, and the suit would be perfect.

She owed it to Andrew to be well dressed, and there were quite a few things she still needed to complete her trousseau.

Still, there was all the next day at her disposal, and if Andrew had finished the business he'd mentioned he might well come with her. He was the kind of man who would have more than a passing interest in what his wife wore.

Bel had asked for her wedding clothes to be delivered straight to Dunbarton Street, but the rest she had

with her as she made her way through the early-
evening throng, looking for a taxi.

That morning, after they had both slept late and
breakfasted together, she had accepted Andrew's offer
to drop her off in Knightsbridge, saying, 'I'll get a cab
back. It will be easier than taking my own car, and
probably quicker in the long run.'

But now with taxi after taxi sailing past occupied,
she was beginning to have doubts.

It had been a long, dry summer, and it was hot and
dusty in the city, the air full of fine grit and exhaust
fumes and the smell of melting tar.

A pigeon swooped between a coach and a van and
hobbled along the gutter like an old lady with bunions
until it reached a squashed ice-cream cone which it
began to peck vigorously.

Well, at least *it* was happy.

Sighing, Bel glanced at her watch. Nearly six-fifteen,
and she could still be standing here in another half an
hour. But the buses were packed and she didn't fancy
the idea of the Underground at rush hour.

She had almost given up hope of getting back in time
to shower and change without being late when a taxi
pulled into the kerb nearby to drop a fare, and she
climbed in thankfully.

'Where to, miss?'

With a strange feeling of unreality, Bel gave the
driver Andrew's Park Lane address.

The uniformed doorman recognised her from the
morning, and as she entered the foyer said a courteous,
'Evening, Miss Grant.'

'Good evening, Rogers.'

Looking gratified that she had remembered his name
from Andrew's brief introduction, he relieved her of

the various packages and, having called the lift, accompanied her up to the penthouse.

When she had opened the door with the key Andrew had provided, Rogers put everything on the couch before hurrying back to his duties.

There wasn't a sound, and the apartment, still not familiar enough to seem like home, had a curiously empty feel. But Andrew would certainly be back by now. He must be showering or getting changed.

Eager to see him and hear his voice, anticipating his kiss, Bel hurried through to the bedroom. But a quick look confirmed that, apart from herself, the penthouse was empty.

She was just digesting that fact when the bedside phone rang.

'Bel?' Above a fair bit of background noise, Andrew sounded abrupt and businesslike. 'I'm sorry. I've been held up and I'm running much later than I'd expected. Can you make your own way to the restaurant?'

'Yes, of course. But I—'

'Bridges is with me, so ask Rogers to get you a cab. See you later.'

Disconcerted, she slowly replaced the receiver, then, gathering herself, she picked it up again and rang down to the foyer.

'I'll have a taxi waiting for you, Miss Grant,' Rogers assured her cheerfully, when she'd made her wants known.

She thanked him and, facing the unwelcome knowledge that she would have to walk into Morro Marengo on her own rather than on Andrew's arm, went to collect her parcels.

He couldn't help being held up, she reminded herself... But it wasn't that, it was his *brusqueness* that hurt.

She had no intention of ever becoming the kind of woman who needed to be handled with kid gloves, but the unwonted prick of tears behind her eyes only served to prove what she already knew: loving Andrew made her vulnerable, made it only too easy for him to wound her.

By the time Bel had showered and dressed she had regained her composure and was ashamed of her own reaction to what, after all, was only a very minor upset.

A touch of lipgloss, her hair taken up in a smooth, shining knot and she was ready, her only jewellery the huge emerald that flashed green fire on her finger.

The black chiffon, she was pleased to see, looked even better than it had in the store. It was the most sophisticated dress she had ever owned. Demurely high at the front, daringly low at the back, its slim skirt slashed almost to the thigh and worn only with a drift of stole, it was stunning in its simplicity.

Sheer black stockings, high-heeled strappy sandals and a small pochette completed the ensemble.

Satisfied she wouldn't disgrace Andrew, and still with a few minutes to spare, she let herself out and went down to the waiting taxi.

When they drew up outside Morro Marengo, she saw Andrew was waiting beneath the pale green and gold canopy. He stepped forward and paid the driver, before opening her door and handing her out.

Still holding her hand, his glance travelled slowly over her slender figure from head to toe before returning to linger on her exquisite face.

The possessive glow in his eyes made her tremble as he raised her hand to his lips and murmured huskily,

'You look absolutely breathtaking... And I'm not even dressed for the occasion.'

The well-cut grey lounge suit he'd left home in that morning was smart enough to be acceptable for any but the most formal gatherings. But, without being in any way fussy, he was fastidious about personal hygiene, and she guessed he would have much preferred to shower and change.

A hand at her waist, he escorted her across the pavement and down the steps that led to the basement restaurant. 'I'm sorry you had to come alone,' he said, 'but I've only just got here myself. How was your day?'

'Highly successful. How was yours?'

'Somewhat less successful,' he answered dryly.

From nowhere came the memory of the previous night's phone call, that somehow familiar voice saying, '...there's been a slip-up...' And Andrew answering, '...I'll deal with it...it shouldn't present any real problem...'

Bel was all at once convinced that it *had*.

Before she could make any comment, or ask any questions, the sight of her father waiting in the lobby put it right out of her mind.

Peter Grant came to meet them, tall and spare, a prepossessing man with a thatch of iron-grey hair and a charming smile.

He was wearing an immaculate dinner jacket, and Bel was pleased to see that he looked quite at home in the understated elegance of his surroundings. Having kissed his cheek, she made the introductions.

As the two men shook hands Andrew apologised with cool civility, 'Forgive me for not being here when you arrived.'

'That's quite all right,' Peter assured him with equal coolness.

'I hope you haven't been waiting long?'

'Only a minute or so.'

'I'd expected to complete some business, but it proved to be impossible and made me too late even to change.'

'A bad day by the sound of it,' the older man commiserated politely.

Sighing inwardly, Bel visualised two dogs warily circling each other, hackles up. Still, it was early days yet.

'What about having a drink in the bar before we go through?' Andrew suggested.

'Oh, yes, that would be lovely,' she agreed brightly. 'Dry sherry for me, please.'

As they stood in the Poseidon bar, sipping their pre-dinner drinks, Peter looked at Andrew levelly and said, 'Bel mentioned that you were a banker.'

'I prefer to think of myself as a businessman.'

Andrew's shoulders lifted in a shrug. 'I have a finger in a great many pies. Television, electronics, property development... I'll take a shot at anything that flies...'

It was obvious that while they were talking the two men were measuring each other up. Peter openly, as was his custom, Andrew more subtly.

Proving that he'd done some checking, Peter remarked, 'I understand your bank backed the prestigious new Calder Development?'

'That's right.'

'And it's turning out to be a goldmine?'

'Right again.'

'Yet you refused to finance a projected development

at Hooton Fen that could have proved just as profitable?'

'There were substantial differences. The former was an inner-city development to resurrect a slum area; the latter was on the edge of a market town and would have meant draining a large area of marshland.'

'An expensive operation, I dare say.'

Almost curtly, Andrew said, 'That area was crucial to wildlife. Building on it would have caused a small, but important ecological disaster. If the developers ever come up with a more suitable site, I may reconsider...'

Recognising that her father had been given the answer he wanted—that Andrew, though a highly successful businessman, was a man who *cared*—Bel relaxed somewhat.

Listening, hoping against hope that they would warm to each other, she watched them as they stood together.

They were both over six feet tall, but her father, nice-looking, uncomplicated, still oddly boyish, his brown eyes bright and intelligent, looked sparer than ever beside Andrew's broad chest and shoulders.

Andrew, formidable, unsmiling, his smoky eyes guarded, looked what he was: a tough, complex man.

An angry man...

Startled by the notion, Bel studied him. Was that undercurrent of simmering anger left over from a frustrating day?

No, she couldn't believe he would allow business aggravations to intrude on his leisure time. His anger, she was oddly certain, was directed against the older man.

But why? Surely he wasn't still annoyed that her father wanted to pay for her wedding clothes?

'About ready to go through?' Andrew's query cut through her uneasy thoughts.

'Yes.' She managed a smile and, slipping one hand through Andrew's arm and the other through her father's, asked gaily, 'What's the betting I'm being escorted by the two handsomest men here?'

'One thing's a cert,' Peter said gallantly, 'we are escorting the most beautiful woman.'

Morro Marengo, Bel soon discovered, wasn't one room but a series of interconnecting cavern-like chambers with arched ceilings.

The decor and lighting had been cleverly, not to say brilliantly done, and gave the most unusual and fascinating effect of an underwater palace lit by multi-drop crystal chandeliers.

When they'd been welcomed and shown to one of the best tables by dark-haired and dapper Luis Morro in person, Peter said, 'As this is a celebration, I hope you will allow me to contribute a bottle of vintage Bollinger?'

'That's very kind of you,' Andrew said smoothly. He turned to Bel. 'Unless you're still off champagne?'

'When did you manage to go off champagne?' her father enquired quizzically.

'At a party one night...' She swallowed. 'I—I drank more than I ought to have done and got up next morning with a hangover.'

The arrival of a waiter with handwritten menus came as a blessed relief. By the time they'd ordered Bel had regained enough composure to steer the conversation into safer channels.

Throughout the meal, which was superb, the two men talked civilly enough and, her fingers crossed, Bel did her utmost to smooth over any awkward moments.

In spite of all her efforts there was an underlying tension that grew abruptly worse when Peter innocently mentioned that her wedding things had been delivered to Dunbarton Street.

'Did you forget your new address?' Andrew's voice was soft as silk, but beneath that bland veneer she knew he was furious.

Meeting and holding his eyes, she said steadily, 'I never got round to telling you, but I'm staying at Dad's tomorrow night.'

'Really? Whose idea was that?'

'Mine.'

'Are you staying there for any particular reason?'

'Because you wanted a traditional wedding, and traditionally the bride should travel to church with her father, or whoever is giving her away, while the groom goes with the best man...'

Drawing a deep breath, she hurried on, 'And on the morning of the wedding it's regarded as unlucky for the bride and groom to see each other until they get to church.'

There was a pregnant silence, then Andrew said, 'Well, in that case, I wouldn't have it any other way.' A shade sardonically, he added, 'If it's a matter of luck, we can't afford to take any chances.'

Peter, who had been sitting silently listening to the little exchange, made some smiling remark about lingering superstitions, and the tension eased.

'So what time can I expect you?' he asked his daughter. Then he added judiciously, 'Or perhaps you could both come to dinner?'

Realising that might be the best way to work things, Bel exclaimed, 'Oh, that would be lovely.'

'I'm afraid you'll have to count me out,' Andrew

said evenly. 'Tomorrow could prove to be another difficult day, and I may not be back until fairly late, but it will save Bel eating alone.'

He appeared to have accepted the arrangements with tolerable good humour, but the evening hadn't gone as well as Bel had hoped and, tired and a little dispirited now, she was glad when the meal was finally over and coffee had been served.

While the men lingered over a brandy she excused herself and went to the pearl and pink powder room, which gave her the subtle impression of being inside a huge, glowing shell.

The place appeared to be empty, but as Bel dried her hands on a pink towel she was joined at the row of gleaming sinks by a slim, petite, redhead wearing an electric blue mini-skirted sheath.

Just as Bel realised who it was their eyes met in the mirror, and Suzy went an unbecoming scarlet.

'Oh, it's *you*,' she muttered. Then, with an attempt to brazen it out she said, 'OK, so it was a rotten thing to do, but all's fair in love and war.'

Turning to look at the other girl, Bel asked the first question that came into her head. 'Is Roderick with you?'

'No, I'm with Freddy Baxter...'

Bel recognised the name. The somewhat effeminate young man was an 'Honourable', the son of one of the Bentincks' aristocratic friends.

'He's broken up with his girlfriend,' Suzy went on, 'and I couldn't turn down the chance of dining at Morro Marengo.' Bitterly, she added, 'The truth is, I was hoping to make Roderick jealous. He hasn't spoken to me since Saturday.'

'I'm sorry about that.'

'Don't be so damned sanctimonious,' Suzy snapped. 'I know you must hate me.'

Bel shook her head. 'I'm very sorry about the way it happened, but I don't hate you.'

'Then you're a fool. I could have stopped it happening, refused to be a party to it. But I never thought you really loved Roderick. *I* love him, and one way or another I intend to get him back—'

She stopped speaking abruptly as Bel moved her hand and the huge emerald on her engagement finger flashed fire.

'My God,' Suzy breathed, staring at it goggle-eyed. 'He told me he wanted you for himself, but though he's a handsome devil, and very charismatic, I never dreamt he'd pull it off this quickly.'

'I don't know what you're talking about,' Bel said stiffly.

'I'm talking about Andrew Storm... It *is* his ring you're wearing?'

The expression on Bel's face was answer enough.

Suzy gave a little crow of laughter. 'You've always looked as if butter wouldn't melt in your mouth, but I'm willing to bet he's already got further with you than Roderick ever did.'

When Bel said nothing, she added with more than a touch of spite, 'I'm forced to admit he's quite a man. But though he wants you now, I should imagine he's the sort that will ditch you as soon as he's had his fun.'

Her mind suddenly ice cold, crystal-clear, Bel asked steadily, 'When did he tell you he wanted me?'

'The night of the party.'

'I didn't realise you knew him.'

'I didn't until that night, though he spoke as if he knew me, so I guess Roderick must have talked about me. The first time I saw Andrew Storm, you and he were dancing together. I watched him kiss you.'

Remembering Suzy's startled face, Bel bit her lip. 'Then what?'

'You still don't know?'

'I thought you might tell me.'

The redhead shrugged. 'Well, if you're sure you want me to...'

But her sherry-coloured eyes were bright with malice, and it was plain that she was only too delighted to have an opportunity to cause further trouble.

'It was later that night and I happened to be at the bar. I saw Andrew Storm pour half a bottle of vodka into a jug of fruit juice. I asked him who he was trying to get sloshed.

'Cool as a cucumber, he said, "Your rival. If you'd like to get Roderick, meet me here in about an hour. I've a proposition to put to you."'

'So you did?'

'Yes... Roderick should have been mine in the first place,' Suzy added defensively.

Refusing to argue, Bel asked, 'What was the proposition?' Though she'd already guessed what it was, somehow she needed to hear it put into words.

'He said that if I helped him, he could—and would—make sure your engagement was broken. I asked him why *he* wanted it broken. That was when he told me he wanted you for himself.'

'And you agreed to help him.' It was a statement, not a question.

Suzy lifted her chin. 'I asked him what he wanted me to do. He told me that you were out for the count and that you'd almost certainly sleep until morning. To make sure you were all right, and in case Roderick did any checking, he intended to sleep in the same room.

'If you showed any signs of waking too early, he'd tap on my door—he already knew my room was just the other side of his—otherwise, at seven-thirty I was to rouse Roderick and bring him to your room.

'I asked if leaving it until the next morning wasn't a bit risky—wouldn't it be better to get it over with straight away?

'But he said no, for two reasons. Firstly it was obvious that you were drunk, and secondly he wanted Roderick to see that you and he had spent the night in the same bed.

'When I asked him how I was supposed to know you were in bed together, he said quite curtly, "Use your imagination. If you can't think of anything better, tell him you were passing the door and you heard a man's voice and peeped in. Even if it's a little…shall we say…*unlikely*, he isn't going to doubt the evidence of his own eyes."'

Nor had he.

Suzy sighed theatrically. 'I suppose knowing that Andrew Storm got you drunk on purpose and planned the whole thing is bound to make a difference to how you feel about him?'

Bel's veneer of composure concealed a quiet, but none the less *burning* anger as she answered coolly, 'You could say that.'

'I for one wouldn't blame you if you never spoke to him again…' she said, and then added with mock sympathy, 'I know it makes you a double loser, but I suppose you'll give him back his ring?'

It was Andrew Bel blamed and was furious with, rather than Suzy, but she was only human, and suddenly she itched to wipe the smirk off the redhead's pretty face.

Holding her temper in check, she said calmly, 'I might just keep it. Knowing the truth makes me feel rather flattered that a man of Andrew's wealth and power should want me enough to go to all that trouble.

'On the other hand, I'm not very happy that Roderick and his parents think so badly of me. So, to set the record straight, I may go to see Roderick and tell him everything you've just told me...'

Suzy's expression changed from triumphant smugness to horror and chagrin as she faced the fact that she might be hoist with her own petard.

'Of course it wouldn't reflect too well on *you*,' Bel went on, 'but I don't care to—'

'You want him back,' Suzy burst out.

'As a matter of fact I don't. But I don't care to be misjudged by people I like and respect.'

Her face red and blotchy, Suzy suddenly looked very young and vulnerable. 'If you tell him, that will be the end of everything. I'll *never* get him. Oh, *please*...' she begged hoarsely.

Though she had no real intention of saying anything, Bel was angry enough not to want to let the girl get off too easily.

'I'll think about it,' she said flatly, and, picking up her small bag, headed for the door.

As if intending to make a further plea, Suzy followed hurriedly at her heels.

An idea forming in her mind, wanting to hit back in some small way, to see Andrew embarrassed, disconcerted, Bel said, 'I'd like you to come and say hello to the folks I'm with.'

Looking uneasy, Suzy agreed, 'All right.'

The men were talking, and the two women had almost reached the table before Andrew glanced up and saw them.

Just for an instant he looked rattled, but his discomfort was swiftly masked and his expression was politely bland as the men rose to their feet with old-fashioned courtesy.

'Look who I've bumped into,' Bel said with assumed brightness. 'Dad, you remember Suzy?'

'Of course.' Peter inclined his head with a charming smile.

'Andrew, you know Suzy, don't you?'

'We have met.' His tone was casual but his eyes were wary. 'How are you, Miss Bainbridge?'

Lacking the *savoir faire* to carry things off, Suzy merely looked uncomfortable.

'I'm sorry I've been such a long time,' Bel apologised, 'but Suzy and I have been having quite a chat.'

'I sometimes wonder what women find to talk about for so long,' Peter remarked humourously.

Bel looked Andrew in the eye and said, 'Men, of course.'

Forcing her to admire his nerve, he laughed. 'It just goes to show how fascinating we are.'

'So are snakes,' she observed sweetly, and caught her father's startled glance.

'I'd better go,' Suzy muttered. 'Freddy will be wondering where I've got to.' Then she whispered to Bel, 'You won't...?'

'No, I won't.'

Her relief unmistakable, Suzy hurried away.

If he was wondering what all that had been about, Peter said nothing.

Still standing, Andrew looked at Bel, and with a wry

twist to his clear-cut lips asked, 'Would you like any more coffee, or are you ready to go?'

'Quite ready,' she told him with brittle politeness.

They made their way to the entrance, to find the grey limousine waiting. Turning to the older man, Andrew queried, 'Can we drop you off?'

After a quick glance at his daughter's set face, Peter shook his head. 'Thanks, but I'll get a taxi.'

Bel kissed his cheek, and promised, 'I'll see you tomorrow.'

The two men shook hands, their leavetaking courteous but lacking warmth.

Ignoring Andrew's proffered hand, Bel climbed into the limousine and settled herself in the far corner. Too angry to make even a pretence at polite conversation, she stayed silent and withdrawn until they reached the Lambeck Building.

Having said goodnight to Bridges, they took the lift up. Though tension crackled between them like electric sparks, neither spoke until they were inside the penthouse.

As soon as the door had closed behind them, Andrew took off his jacket and tossed it over a chair, then, loosening his tie, he turned to face her, tall and dark and intimidating, overwhelmingly masculine.

Bel stared at him in silence while the adrenalin pumped through her veins.

'Would you like a nightcap?' he asked coolly.

'No.' She made no attempt at civility now.

He wore a deliberating look, the expression of a man weighing up the opposition, wondering how best to deal with it.

After a moment or two, with an air of patient reasonableness that infuriated her, he said, 'Perhaps you'd like to tell me why you're upset?'

Oh, but he was a master tactician, she thought bitterly, playing it cool, giving nothing away just in case she hadn't learnt the whole truth.

'Don't you know?' Her manner was taut, strained from holding back the build-up of anger and resentment.

'I can't imagine,' he assured her, with little conviction and even less truth.

'And I can't imagine why I ever agreed to marry a man who is a rogue and a liar, rotten to the core and totally unscrupulous.'

When, his face impassive, he said nothing, she cried, angered afresh, 'You got me drunk purposely... You planned the whole thing without caring two hoots how much you upset Roderick or his parents... And you certainly weren't worried about shaming and degrading me. You made me feel like some cheap tramp—'

'I'm sorry about that.' His voice was cool, incisive. 'But I couldn't let you go ahead and marry totally the wrong man.'

'Who gave you the right to decide he was the wrong man?' she demanded wrathfully.

'Well, wasn't he?'

When she refused to answer, Andrew went on, 'I knew you were the woman for me. I had to bring that engagement to an end somehow.'

'Did you have to be quite so brutal about it? Why couldn't you have tried...well...being nice to me?'

'The old-fashioned term is wooing,' he pointed out succinctly.

'Well, any other man would have—'

'But I'm not "any other man..."' He took her upper

arms in a light grip. 'And if I had tried to woo you, how far would that have got me? You're not the kind of woman who would have entertained another man while you were engaged to Bentinck.'

'But what you did was so *heartless*...'

'They were desperate measures, I admit, but time was getting short.'

When he would have drawn her closer, she pulled herself loose and turned away, her shining head bent. Her mood had changed, and from being furiously angry she now felt drained, on the verge of tears.

'Come on, Bel,' he coaxed, his eyes on the purity of her profile. 'Don't let's quarrel. What's done can't be undone. It's better to let it go. You've admitted you wouldn't go back to Bentinck. You're wearing my ring, not his, and in less than forty-eight hours we'll be married.'

'What you mean is, you're satisfied you've won...'

There was something about the way she spoke that made him look at her warily.

'And you believe the end justifies the means? Well, I don't!' Huskily, she went on, 'I'm no longer sure I want to marry you.'

She started to take off the emerald, sliding it over her knuckle. 'As for your ring, I don't want to wear it any more until—' She stopped with a gasp as, seizing her hand, he thrust the ring back, holding it in place with a grip that threatened to break her delicate bones.

Raising her chin, she looked him in the face. 'You're hurting me. Please let me go.' In spite of all her efforts her voice shook.

His eyes hard as grey granite, he said, 'Then leave the ring where it is.'

When she stood quietly, making no further move to take it off, his grip slackened and he released her hand.

Nursing it, she turned away, informing him stiffly, 'I'm going to bed now, and I'm moving into one of the guest rooms.'

Catching her arm, he swung her to face him and took her shoulders in a grip just short of brutal. 'I'm damned if you are! You made your choice and you're sticking with it.'

Though the words were spoken softly, the underlying hint of violence made her shiver. Still she defied him. 'What I've learnt has made me change my mind. I've no intention of sleeping with you tonight. I need a chance to think things over.'

She saw his face darken with fury, but, refusing to be cowed, she added levelly, 'If you insist on us sharing a bed, then I'll walk out of here right now and take a taxi to Dunbarton Street.'

His eyes flashed, and, knowing she'd pushed him too far, she held her breath while she waited for the explosion.

It was a moment electric with tension; she could feel the build-up of fury and exasperation, the tautness in his lean, powerful-body.

But his excellent self-control held, and after a moment, his face schooled into a dispassionate mask, he released her shoulders and said calmly, 'Very well. But you stay where you are. I'll be the one to move out.'

Reaction made her legs feel like jelly as, without a word, she turned and headed for the safety of a solitary bed.

CHAPTER NINE

HER cases still hadn't been unpacked and, unwilling to sleep in the nude, as she had done the previous night, Bel searched for something to wear. She came up with a shortie nightshirt that Ellen had bought her last Christmas.

While she showered and cleaned her teeth, and brushed her long hair, her agitated thoughts went batting backwards and forwards like a bumblebee.

Could she still marry Andrew, knowing how devious he could be, how unscrupulous? He had acted in a way that proved he could be both cruel and ruthless, and she couldn't believe the end justified the means.

Yet she was convinced that basically he wasn't a cruel man, and, though at the moment she was upset and furious with him, she knew he was kind and caring and had his own strong principles.

And he'd been right about her not being the kind of woman who would have entertained another man while she was still engaged to Roderick...

Poor Roderick, he didn't deserve to be hurt and humiliated, to have his hopes and dreams destroyed so callously.

Yet if Andrew hadn't used those bulldozing tactics she would have almost certainly gone ahead and married him, and it would have been a sad mistake.

Oh, they might have rubbed along comfortably

enough, but Roderick would have been cheated out of the most precious gift a man could have: a wife who truly, *ardently* loved him.

While she, without that divine spark, that passionate love Andrew had kindled, would never have reached the heights, never have been completely fulfilled.

So how could she go on agonising over it?

Nothing could change what had happened, and though in some ways she longed to set the record straight she could see no point in causing Roderick any further heartache. And she had promised Suzy.

Nor—she faced the truth squarely—did she want this knowledge to wreck her future relationship with Andrew. Though without his love their marriage would be incomplete, it offered her only chance of happiness.

Going back to the empty bedroom, she climbed into bed with a sigh. Her self-respect had demanded a show-down, and she should be pleased she'd won the battle. But, no longer buoyed up by righteous anger and indignation, she felt no sense of satisfaction or elation, only desolation and sadness.

She wanted to be in his arms where she belonged, not sleeping alone. A wave of longing engulfed her and she bit her lip. But she wouldn't go to him; her pride wouldn't allow it.

Pride was a chilly, uncomfortable bedfellow, her mother had used to say, not one to be encouraged...

Bel was out of bed and on her way to the door when a thought stopped her in her tracks. Andrew wasn't a man to be trifled with. What if he was still angry? What if he looked at her coldly and rejected her?

The possibility shrivelled her courage, and she was retreating back to bed when there was a sudden tap at the door. She gave a startled glance over her shoulder.

Andrew, fresh from the shower, his feet and legs bare, was wearing a short white towelling robe. He looked strong and virile and beautiful, and she quivered as though her entire being belonged to him.

'I came to say goodnight.' He spoke to her half-turned back, his voice, though holding no trace of anger, cool and remote. 'I have to make an early start in the morning, so I may not see you.'

'Oh…' It was a forlorn little whisper of sound that got lost in the silence. Taking a deep breath, she said carefully, 'Then I'll see you in church.'

She sensed his relief before he murmured, 'Well, goodnight, Bel.'

'Andrew…'

He paused, and she felt his utter stillness.

Wondering how best to break the ice, she turned to look at him.

Perhaps reading her change of heart in her face, he opened his arms, and she walked into them like someone going home.

But when she stood on tiptoe and lifted her face to kiss him, instead of meeting her lips he moved his head back with great deliberation and looked down at her.

Something about his considering look made her uncomfortable. 'Don't you want me to kiss you?'

Coolly he told her, 'It seems a shame not to take up an offer like that, but the trouble about kissing is that it almost invariably leads to other things… And you did say you had no intention of sleeping with me tonight…'

'Until I'd had a chance to think things over.'

'Have you had a chance?'

'Yes.'

'And what have you decided?'

'To take your advice and forget the past.'

She saw by the flare of satisfaction in his eyes it was what he'd hoped to hear. But it wasn't until he said mockingly, 'In that case, you can kiss me,' that she realised he intended to make her pay for her earlier stand.

Her soft mouth tightening, she said, 'I'm no longer sure I want to.'

'Oh, but I'm sure *I* want *you* to.'

He ran his fingers into her thick, silky hair and, holding her head between his long, well-shaped hands, drew her lips towards his until they almost touched.

When she made no attempt to kiss him, he tilted her head back, leaving her slim throat vulnerable to the ravages of his lips and teeth and tongue.

She gasped and shivered as his mouth grazed over the soft skin beneath her jaw and lingered at the hollow behind her ear. But there was something about him, a hint of violence, that, though held strictly in check, warned her not to struggle.

When his mouth finally closed over hers, his kiss was harsh, punitive, until finally it gave way to a deep, sensuous exploration. Head spinning, she leaned limply against him. It wasn't so much surrender as a merciless subjugation.

While he kissed her one skilled hand began to rove over her body, cupping the weight of her breast, teasing a nipple, then following the curve of her hip to locate and exploit an even more sensitive spot.

His mouth moved to find her breast and she shuddered and arched towards him. It was ravishment, pure and simple.

Desire ran through her, wave after wave of it, submerging her defences and dragging her under like some powerful undertow.

By the time he picked her up and put her on the bed she was taut with wanting. When, having tossed aside the towelling robe, he joined her, with a need, an urgency that wouldn't be denied, she pulled him down to her.

But after he'd lowered himself into the cradle of her hips and with a single strong thrust made their two bodies one, with fine self-control he paused and waited.

When her lids flew open, he smiled at her and said, 'This time I want to look into your eyes while I'm making love to you, to see exactly what I'm doing to you.'

His gaze holding hers, he began to move with long, slow, deliberate thrusts, stopping only when she closed her eyes again. She felt that he was looking into her very soul.

'Look at me,' he ordered softly.

When she obeyed, appalled by this fine edge of cruelty, this need to dominate, but caught up in a wanting that wouldn't be denied, he began to build a tightening coil of sensation that gradually engulfed her whole body.

Then, having kept her poised on the brink until he'd wrung from her inarticulate whimpers and moans and gasps, he sent her tumbling over the edge, and while the tremors of ecstasy still spread through her in golden spirals he followed her.

Looking into his eyes while he'd made love to her seemed to have made her wholly his. It was the most overwhelming experience she had ever known, and she knew that if he left her now she would want to die.

But when he'd lifted himself away, he drew her into

his arms and, with a kind of tenderness that wiped out his previous cruelty, settled her head on his chest.

It was bliss. Contentment. Home.

Euphoric, she drifted into a deep and dreamless sleep.

When she awoke it was broad daylight and she was alone in the big, comfortable bed. The light curtains were billowing in a warm breeze coming through the open window, and she could hear, far below, the muted roar of traffic moving along Park Lane.

A glance at her watch showed it was nearly eight-thirty, and the silence made it clear that Andrew had already gone.

She had hoped to wake in time to see him, perhaps even to make love again. Now, though she knew it was quite ridiculous, she felt the emptiness, the sense of loss she always experienced whenever he left her.

There was a note propped up on the bedside table. Sitting back against the pillows, she unfolded the single sheet of paper covered in Andrew's black positive scrawl, and read:

I didn't want to leave you. You were sleeping like a babe and didn't stir when I kissed you...which was just as well. If you'd put your arms around my neck and kissed me back, I might have found it impossible to tear myself away.

I forgot to mention we'll be going on honeymoon straight after the reception, so when you've finished buying your trousseau, pack a case and take it with you.

See you in church.
Andrew.

She read it twice, happy at the thought of a honeymoon, even happier that he hadn't wanted to leave her.

Last night, when he'd cradled her head against his chest, he'd seemed almost tender. Was it possible he was starting to feel something for her?

Jumping out of bed, her spirits soaring, she pulled on a robe and went through to the kitchen to make herself coffee and toast.

By a quarter to ten she was in a taxi heading for Harrods. She bought, amongst other things, a selection of mix-and-match skirts and tops, a seductive nightdress and negligee, some cobwebby underwear and a modest matching set of luggage. Before four-thirty her trousseau shopping was completed.

Andrew wouldn't be home, and with everything she needed already dispatched to Dunbarton Street she could see no point going back to his empty apartment.

Feeling the need for some fresh air and exercise after spending nearly the whole day in a crowded store, she set off to walk to the Grant Filey offices. Her father would still be there and they could go home together.

The afternoon was warm and sunny, and, avoiding other pedestrians with the ease that came of practice, she walked briskly, her thoughts keeping pace with her steps.

It scarcely seemed possible that in just a few days her life had changed so dramatically, that tomorrow she was getting married to a man she loved with the kind of overwhelming passion she had never imagined herself capable of.

A man who might be starting to love her...

Suddenly she wanted to sing and dance and shout her happiness from the rooftops. With a sudden excess of *joie de vivre* she gave an impulsive little skip, like a lamb gambolling in spring meadows, and when a complete stranger smiled at her she smiled back without embarrassment.

When she reached the offices and put her head round her father's door he was still behind his desk.

Looking surprised, he said, 'I didn't expect to see you quite this early.'

'Having spent all your money, I thought I'd beg a lift back with you.' Her smile and her voice reflected her high spirits.

He beamed, and, recalling the previous night and the uncomfortable undercurrents, she guessed he was relieved.

'I'll be through in a minute,' he told her. 'I'm just waiting for the latest accounts figures from Harmen.'

'In that case I'll ask Rosie to get me a cup of tea.' Bel made herself scarce.

It was almost half an hour later, and Rosie and the rest of the staff had gone home, before her father appeared in the outer office, a faint frown drawing his brows together.

'Something wrong?' Bel asked as they made their way to the small car park at the rear.

His frown deepened. 'A discrepancy between the bank's figures and ours. Harmen is going to check it out first thing tomorrow and give me a ring.'

They had joined the early-evening traffic and were on their way to Dunbarton Street before a thought occurred to Bel, and she remarked, 'Speaking of checking... Last night I got the impression you'd been doing some of your own?'

'Yes, I had,' Peter admitted.

'What did you discover about Andrew?'

Her father replied without hesitation. 'As you mentioned, he guards his privacy and there's little known of his personal life, but his business reputation is impeccable. He's noted for being shrewd and far from soft, and for having an almost uncanny ability to make money. But it's also universally acknowledged that he's scrupulously fair and honest.'

'Then you're feeling happier about the wedding?'

'So long as you love each other... By the way, have you any plans for afterwards?'

'Andrew said we'd be going straight off on honeymoon, though he didn't say where.'

'He's keeping the destination a secret, eh?' With a reminiscent smile, Peter recalled, 'I remember trying to surprise your mother...'

Having packed, and laid out her wedding things ready for the morning, Bel was in bed by ten-thirty that night. Excitement kept her awake, however, and she lay and listened to the church clock chime away the hours until dawn was fingering the sky.

A shaft of bright sunlight shining through a slit in the curtains wakened her. She had just stirred and stretched when there was a knock, and Mrs Piggot appeared with a tray of tea.

'Didn't want you to sleep too late,' she said cheerfully. 'It's going to be a lovely day, so I wondered if you'd like the buffet set on the terrace?'

'Oh, yes, that would be lovely.'

As the housekeeper bustled out she turned to say, 'If you need any help with your dress or anything, just let me know.'

'Yes, I will.' Bel smiled her thanks.

In the event everything went smoothly, and with her

hair taken up in a shining knot, she was dressed and waiting in the living room in plenty of time.

A Mayfair florist had delivered an exquisite bouquet of dark red scented rosebuds from Andrew, and the door had barely closed when the bell pealed again to announce the arrival of the wedding car.

'I'd better go and tell your father.' Mrs Piggot was breathless with excitement. 'He's been on the telephone and he's running late.'

A few seconds later Peter hurried in. Taking Bel's hands, he said, 'You look absolutely lovely.'

She gave him a hug, and, having pulled her veil into place, picked up her bouquet and allowed him to escort her out to the white-ribboned car.

The church was small and beautiful, the sunshine slanting through its mellow stained glass making jewelled patterns on the polished pews and the worn red carpet. There were fresh flowers everywhere and the organist was quietly playing Wagner.

The matron of honour, a slender, dark-haired girl wearing a simple champagne-coloured dress, hovered uncertainly while Andrew, with his best man, waited at the chancel steps.

He turned to watch her walk up the aisle on her father's arm, and Bel saw that he looked handsome as Lucifer in a lightweight suit and immaculate white shirt, a carnation in his buttonhole.

When she reached his side he smiled down at her, but his eyes held the possessive gleam that she knew and recognised rather than the love she'd hoped for.

The Reverend John Blackthorn, tall and balding, welcomed them with a smile, and, having collected the little group with a practised eye, began the short ceremony.

All the responses were made clearly, and the matron of honour was at hand to take Bel's bouquet. The only surprise was when the best man produced not one wedding band but two, and Bel found herself putting a thick gold ring on Andrew's finger.

As soon as the register had been signed, the vicar thanked and a few photographs taken, Andrew helped his bride into the wedding car.

Apart from a brief kiss at the end of the ceremony he had scarcely glanced at her, and during the short drive he didn't say a word. Disconcerted by his air of cool aloofness, she too remained silent until they reached Dunbarton Street.

By the time they got out of the car, the others were drawing up. Peter welcomed the slimly built, fair-haired best man and his wife, kissed his daughter and shook hands with his new son-in-law before saying heartily, 'Let's go through and see if we can do justice to Mrs Piggot's spread.'

He had just ushered them onto the sunny terrace and started to open a bottle of champagne when the phone rang.

There was no sign of the housekeeper, so Bel, who was standing close to the French windows, went to pick up the receiver.

'Peter?' The voice at the other end was familiar. 'I've done the checking you asked me to do. There still seems to be a bit of a problem, so I'll need more time...'

Bel was standing there frozen when her father appeared. 'Harmen?' he queried.

She nodded mutely.

Taking the phone from her nerveless fingers, Peter listened for a moment, then said briskly, 'I talked to

Hargreaves earlier and he'd like to look at our books. I've given him the go-ahead and he's sending one of his accountants over, name of Lombard...'

Without looking to where Andrew was standing, just beyond the French windows, Bel was aware that he was listening to the conversation.

'He should be with you shortly. Yes...show him anything he wants to see. I'll be in myself later this afternoon...' Replacing the receiver, Peter said cheerfully, 'Now for that champagne...'

Moving like an automaton, Bel followed her father back to the terrace and accepted a glass of the sparkling wine. She felt shocked and dazed, thoughts ricocheting in her mind.

When she'd answered the phone at Andrew's penthouse that first night the caller had sounded oddly familiar. Now she knew why. The voice on the other end of the line had been Harmen's.

Yet when she'd asked Andrew if he knew their company secretary, he'd said no...

But he'd been lying!

Suddenly the pieces of the jigsaw dropped into place. The day they had first met, in the restaurant, he had been Harmen's companion at lunch. That was why the back of his dark head had looked familiar.

Bel's throat went dry. Why was he in contact with Harmen? What on earth was he up to?

A feeling of panic gripped her and her heart began to race. What kind of man had she married? Someone underhand and dishonest she could neither trust nor respect?

Taking a deep breath, she struggled for calm. The last time she'd had reason to doubt Andrew's personal morals instead of *asking* she'd jumped to a conclusion which had proved to be wrong.

So what about his business morals?

She thought of her father's verdict. '…his business reputation is impeccable…it's acknowledged that he's scrupulously fair and honest…'

If that was the truth, and she had no reason to doubt it, there must be an innocent reason for Andrew concealing the fact that he knew Harmen.

Making an effort to fight down her uneasiness, Bel told herself firmly that this was her wedding day and she didn't want to spoil it. So, until she could speak to Andrew in private, ask for an explanation, she would push the matter to the back of her mind…

Looking up, she met his brilliant gaze, and with a little shock realised he'd been studying her with the penetrating scrutiny that seemed to see right into her head.

After holding her eyes for a moment, he glanced from her to her father and said casually, 'It's high time I introduced my stepbrother properly. Bel… Peter… this is Jonathan Filey.'

While Bel stood quiet and unmoving, her mind reeling from the shock, Peter asked, 'Conrad Filey's son?'

'That's right.'

Andrew had told her his mother had married a second time, and to a London businessman, Bel thought dazedly, but he'd hidden the fact that her second husband had been Conrad Filey.

Looking startled, Peter said, 'Well, this *is* a surprise.' Then to Jonathan he said, 'I was sorry to hear that both your father and stepmother had died in that big hotel fire.'

'It came as a shock to lose them both,' Jonathan admitted.

He was young, no more than twenty-one or two, with a thin face and intelligent blue eyes. He shook Peter's outstretched hand, then with a glance at Andrew queried, 'Mind if I kiss the bride?'

'Feel free.' Andrew gave his permission ironically.

Touching his lips to Bel's frozen cheek, Jonathan observed, 'Andrew's a very lucky man.'

'Thank you.' Somehow she managed a smile.

Brows drawn together in a frown, Peter asked his daughter, 'Why didn't you tell me Andrew was Conrad's stepson?'

Feeling as though she'd been hit by a bus, Bel admitted, 'I had no idea he was.'

Jonathan took the hand of the pretty dark-haired girl who was standing by his side. 'This is my wife, Penny. We haven't been married very long ourselves...'

While the conversation went on around her Bel struggled to come to terms with this latest bombshell.

What kind of game was Andrew playing? A few days ago he'd made a point of asking her what she'd thought of Conrad Filey, but he'd said absolutely nothing about knowing him or being related to him in any way.

Why had he wanted to keep it a secret? Though he was a many-faceted man, with a complex mind, she couldn't see him doing it just to amaze. He must have had a cogent reason...

Another and more puzzling thought struck her. Having kept it a secret, why had he chosen to spring it on them in this way...?

Disturbing thoughts jostling in her mind, Bel made a pretence of eating. She even managed to smile and join in the conversation from time to time, as though nothing was amiss, in spite of a growing conviction that something was terribly wrong.

It came as a relief when, after a glance at his watch, Andrew remarked, 'If we're going to make it to the airport, I suggest you get changed.'

'Do you need any help?' Penny asked diffidently.

'Oh, yes, please.' Bel smiled at the girl, who looked little more than eighteen, and, leaving the three men talking, led the way to her bedroom.

As Penny helped her out of the rustling wedding dress and into the mink-coloured silk suit Bel remarked, 'Jonathan said you hadn't been married very long…?'

'Just a month,' the girl admitted, blushing.

'How well do you know Andrew?'

'Not very well, really. He came to our wedding, but apart from that we've only met once or twice. To tell you the truth I find him rather…well, intimidating.'

'Yes, he can be.'

'Even Jonny seems a bit overawed at times.'

'Of course, there's a fairly big age-gap,' Bel remarked encouragingly.

'Almost ten years. And they've never been what you might call close. Andrew was grown up and travelling round the world by the time his mother married Jonny's father. It's only recently that Andrew's kind of taken Jonny under his wing. When his parents died in that awful fire, Jonny was still at college. There wasn't any money, and things were very difficult…'

Then, in a burst of confidence, Penny rushed on, 'You see we hadn't intended to get married until next year, then we found we *had* to… But Andrew's been very good to us both. He paid for the wedding, found

Jonny a job in his bank and bought us a house for a wedding present. That's why we were so pleased when he told us he was getting married. He deserves to be happy—'

There was a tap at the door and Mrs Piggot put her head round. 'Mr Storm said to tell you that your cases are in the car and you've only just time to get to the airport.'

'We'll be straight down,' Bel promised.

When she'd adjusted the tangerine silk scarf that looped loosely round her throat and floated over her shoulders, she gave Penny an impulsive hug. 'Thank you for your help... Oh, and even though you're already married I'd still like you to have this.' She handed the girl her bouquet.

'How lovely.' Penny looked delighted. As they hurried out she added with shy smile, 'I suppose in a roundabout way we're related...sort of stepsisters-in-law.'

Andrew was waiting in the hall, his strong face impassive. If he was impatient he showed no sign of it as he watched the two women descend the stairs.

When they reached the bottom he held out a lean, strong hand to Bel. With a feeling that verged on reluctance, she put hers into it.

Peter and Jonathan appeared, and, after an exchange of hugs and kisses and handshakes on the doorstep, the newly-weds were showered with rose petals and waved off.

Needing desperately to talk to Andrew, to be given some kind of reassurance, Bel turned to him. But his eyes held a cool warning and she became aware that the limousine's glass panel, which allowed Bridges to hear, was open.

Andrew made no effort to close it. Realising it was a refusal to discuss things at this juncture, Bel bit her lip, scared and angry, and stared out of the window at the passing traffic.

After watching her half-averted face for a while, he said, 'You haven't asked where we're going.'

She said nothing, and he went on, 'I thought a few days in Rome first and then a trip to Venice?'

When she still failed to reply, he reached for her hand and held it, his thumb pressing into the soft palm in a tacit warning that he expected her to follow his lead.

'Have you ever been to Venice?'

'No.'

'It's a most beautiful, romantic city. Ideal for a honeymoon…'

As things stood she had no intention of honeymooning in Venice, or anywhere else for that matter. Before the marriage was consummated, before she was caught and trapped in that web of sexual excitement he spun so effortlessly, she needed answers to a lot of questions.

CHAPTER TEN

WHEN they reached the Villa Dolce far Niente it was early evening and, though it was still warm and sunny, the burning heat of the day was over.

They climbed the stairs together, yet apart, and Andrew carried their luggage into the bedroom while Bel, taut and on edge, went through to the living room.

The windows onto the terrace were thrown wide and a huge jug of fresh flowers stood in the hearth, but there was no sign of the housekeeper.

'I told Maria not to stay,' Andrew remarked from the doorway. 'As it's our honeymoon I thought it would be nice to have the place to ourselves.' Then he added blandly, 'Why don't you make yourself at home while I fix us a cool drink?'

Sitting down on the settee, looking around a room that she was forced to admit was even more pleasant than she remembered, Bel made a determined but unsuccessful effort to relax.

The relatively short flight from London had been smooth and without incident, and during the journey, following the lead Andrew had forced on her, she had made polite conversation.

Just as though they were virtual strangers, she thought bitterly, rather than newly-weds.

But, while appearing outwardly cool and composed, a growing realisation of just what kind of game

Andrew must have been playing had made the tension mount. It stoked the fires of anger and apprehension and built up a dangerous pressure, making her head ache and her stomach churn.

Andrew returned, moving lightly, and handed her a tall frosted glass of fruit juice. He had discarded his jacket and looked coolly elegant in casual trousers and a dark silk shirt and tie.

While he drained his glass he stood silently, looking out across the sun-warmed rooftops of Rome towards the river.

When his glass was empty he put it on the table alongside hers and, using one hand to loosen the knot in his tie, came to sit beside her.

Only when she pointedly moved away did Bel realise that though Andrew *looked* relaxed, he was actually as tense as she herself.

Grasping her upper arms, he jerked her towards him and, staring down into her scared but defiant eyes, said with soft violence, 'I refuse to be treated as though I'm some kind of leper. I'm your husband and—'

Tearing herself free, she jumped to her feet and whirled to face him. 'I'll tell you exactly what you are. You're a despicable, scheming, unprincipled, lying swine! You told me you didn't know Mortimer Harmen. But you were lunching with him the day I bumped into you and he was the man who phoned your penthouse that night. Don't try to deny it!'

'I wasn't going to deny it. And I'm sorry I had to lie to you.'

'Oh, I just bet you are!'

'I kept to the truth whenever possible.'

'You wouldn't recognise the truth if it came up and bit you,' she cried contemptuously. 'But don't bother telling me any more lies. It's obvious Harmen's been giving you information, and—'

She broke off abruptly as realisation dawned. 'He was the one who told you I'd gone to Italy!'

'Yes. Your father mentioned it to him and said you'd be staying at the company's flat. I was heading for your apartment that morning when I caught sight of that young ruffian attempting to steal your bag.'

So that explained it! 'And Harmen's been helping you to try to take over Dad's firm, hasn't he? What did you offer him? A free rein? A directorship?'

'Something along those lines—plus a substantial cash payment when I'd gained control of the company. I had him checked out and discovered he was exceedingly fond of wine, women and song, so it was easy to bribe him.'

Andrew's calm admission was like a kick in the stomach. Some part of her, perhaps the part that loved him, had clung to the hope that he would deny the charges, explain away his apparent involvement.

She sat down abruptly on an old wheel-backed chair and folded her arms across her stomach, as though to hold back the pain. 'Why do you want Grant Filey? As far as you're concerned it's insignificant—a mere drop in the ocean...'

But even as she asked she knew the answer. 'You don't want it... You just want to get back at Dad for something...' She was feeling her way now, thinking aloud. 'Something that's happened in the past... Something you think he's done to your stepfather... That's why you kept the relationship a secret, why you introduced your stepbrother in the way you did. You wanted to throw Dad. But you didn't succeed. And you won't succeed in gaining control of his company either.'

'I already have.'

The quiet assertion rocked her. Then she rallied. 'You can't have gained a controlling interest without Ellen's shares.'

'They were signed over to me yesterday.'

'I don't believe a word of it. She's in France, probably at Épernay with a man named Jean-Claude...'

'When your stepmother first agreed to sell her shares I arranged an all-expenses-paid trip to Paris as a kind of bonus.'

As Bel's jaw dropped he went on relentlessly, 'I have a champagne house at Épernay with a distribution set-up in Paris. Jean-Claude works in my Champs-Élysées offices. He was more than happy to pay court to a beautiful blonde for a while.'

'You wanted her kept out of the way!'

'For more than one reason,' Andrew admitted coolly. 'Though unfortunately the plan backfired, and caused me a great deal of trouble...'

Bel was just beginning to get an inkling of what he was about to tell her when he went on, 'Working undercover, Harmen had bought up all the shares he could get his hands on, but I still needed your stepmother's to give me control. To absolve her from any blame, she parted with them believing the company was buying them back. Then Harmen came across a paper she'd somehow omitted to sign...'

Yes, Bel could hear the voice she'd later recognised as Harmen's saying, 'I've just discovered there's been a slip-up...'

'I went over to Épernay to rectify matters, only to find Jean-Claude had exceeded his orders and taken your stepmother off somewhere. I waited as long as I dared, but when they hadn't returned by teatime I had no option but to come back and try again the next day.'

That explained his being nearly late for dinner, and why he'd been so tied up the following day. But there was still one thing she didn't understand.

'If you thought you already had control, why was it necessary to keep Ellen out of the way?'

Then, with a sudden blinding flash of knowledge, she went on, 'No, don't bother to tell me. I know. It was so she wouldn't speak to Dad and the truth wouldn't come out until after the wedding. *You wanted a complete take-over: the company and me...*'

It was so; she was sure of it. It explained his determined pursuit and why he'd gone to such lengths to break up her engagement.

Still she shook her head, dissatisfied. Why had he included *her* in the take-over? If it had simply been a wife he'd wanted there were plenty of women more suited to his world—beautiful, intelligent, sophisticated women...

'Why *me*?'

'Don't you know?'

Suddenly she did. Through a dry throat, she said, 'Because Dad loves me, and for whatever reason you were determined to take everything away from him.'

Andrew sighed. 'It began that way, but I—'

Eyes flashing, she broke in, 'Didn't it occur to you that when I found out just what your motives were I would walk out? Or did you think I was so...obsessed by you that I would forgive you anything?'

Before he could answer, she went on raggedly, 'I see now why you wanted me to love you. The bonds of love are even stronger than the bonds of passion.' Panic brought her to her feet. 'Well, you may have the company, but you won't have me. I'm going straight back to London and I intend to get a divorce as soon as possible.'

It was a moment of electric tension, and she felt the coiled reaction in his lean, powerful body.

Head back, eyes narrowed to gleaming blue-grey slits between thick dark lashes, he looked up at her. 'On what grounds?' he asked silkily. 'If you were thinking of non-consummation...?'

Her face betrayed her.

'I'm afraid not, my darling wife. As an eager bridegroom I've waited long enough. I was just about to take you to bed.'

'Now I know how vile you are, I wouldn't sleep with you if you were the last man on earth,' she spat at him. 'I can't bear the idea of you touching me.'

He was on his feet, his face taut with anger. 'I intend to do a great deal more than merely touch you.'

Before she had realised his intention, he'd swept her up into his arms and was carrying her through to the bedroom.

Furiously she strove to free herself, but he held her easily in spite of her struggles. Pushing the door closed with his foot, he dropped her onto the bed.

'No...' she begged huskily.

But he was drawing her close and, his lips brushing her ear, telling her that she was beautiful, exquisite...whispering how he loved to feel her nipples firm beneath his touch, how it excited him to put his face against the silky softness of her breast and take the rosy peak in his mouth, how it felt when the warmth of her body welcomed his and how mind-blowing it was to make love to her and feel her response deep inside...

Within seconds she was lost.

Using only his voice and the mental images he created, he set her alight and made her want him with a fierce passion that obliterated past and future, that wiped out reason and thought and left only feeling.

Bel awoke to the bright sunshine of early morning and a dark despair.

How could she have succumbed to Andrew's sexual blandishments and allowed the marriage to be consummated?

But the earth-shattering feelings he'd aroused had been so strong, the delight and ecstasy she'd experienced so consuming...

Now the bitterness she felt was in direct proportion to the previous night's pleasure, wiping it out as if it had never been, leaving only burning anger and futile regrets.

He'd just wanted to use her as a means of hurting her father, and she felt sick when she recalled how she had hoped and longed for his love. He felt nothing for her and never would.

Yet they were lying as if they belonged together, two halves of a whole. Her knees were drawn up, her buttocks fitting snugly into the warm curve of his abdomen and thighs. She was conscious of the slight rise and fall of his chest against her back, and the weight of his arm lying across her ribs.

This mockery of loving intimacy was like a knife twisting cruelly in her heart. Perhaps she made some sound of pain because she felt the breath of his waking sigh stir her hair.

A moment later the arm lying across her ribs moved slightly, and a warm hand closed possessively round her breast and began to tease the nipple.

After all he'd done to her, the casual insolence of his touch was like a spark to dynamite.

With a sudden savage jerk she tore herself free, and turning on her knees, angry beyond words, came back fighting. The flat of her hand swung in an arc and hit his cheek with a resounding crack.

Taken by surprise by such totally out-of-character behaviour, he was fractionally slow in reacting. As he sat up, and before he had made any real attempt to defend himself, she went for him with unrestrained fury.

'I h-hate you!' She was half sobbing, almost incoherent with rage. 'And if you think I'm going to stay with you...'

He caught her wrists, but the force of her onslaught carried them both backwards and off the bed.

There was no carpet, only polished floorboards, but, throwing his arms around her protectively, he rolled like a judo black belt, minimising the impact.

'You little wildcat,' he muttered. Capturing both hands, he forced them above her head and, pinning her beneath him, used the weight of his body to hold her there.

'Let me go,' she gasped, struggling furiously. 'I want to get up.'

He was breathing quickly, a lock of dark hair falling over his forehead, but his voice was steady as he told her, 'I have every intention of keeping you right where you are until you've calmed down.'

Stooping, he lifted her back onto the bed and got in beside her. Gathering herself, her only thought to get as far away from him as possible, she made an effort to slip out at the far side.

His fingers closed around her arm, holding her back. 'Don't go. I want to talk to you.'

She bit on her soft inner lip until she tasted blood. 'Please take your hands off me.'

'Not until you agree to stay and listen to what I have to say.'

'I don't want to talk to you.' Her beautiful mouth set in a stubborn line.

He was a wily tactician, and he said with conscious generosity, 'I'm not looking for an apology—'

'What a pity,' she broke in, 'because I'm just *dying* to give you one.'

Ignoring the sarcasm, he went on, 'But I think we need to talk to clear the air. I want to know why you flew at me.'

Such barefaced provocation took her breath away. 'Are you saying I haven't reason enough?'

His voice like polished steel, he asked, 'For behaving like an alley cat?'

A compulsion stronger than her will made her look at him. Resentful that, after all he'd done, he was making her feel in the wrong, she muttered, 'You asked for it.' But her voice lacked conviction, and all at once she was desperately ashamed of her own behaviour.

'I'm sorry,' she muttered. Then, very close to tears, she went on, 'But I didn't want this—' her gesture took in the pair of them in bed together '—to happen…I can't bear to stay with you knowing why you married me…'

'But you *don't* know why I married you.'

'You admitted it was to get back at Dad for something.'

'No, I said it *began* that way. Look, I'll start from the beginning, if you're prepared to listen?'

When he made as if to cuddle her against him, she moved away as far as the bed would allow.

'I'll listen,' she agreed stiffly, 'but then I intend to leave.'

'Very well.' His face set, the tanned skin taut over the strong bone structure, he admitted defeat. 'If you still feel the same when you've heard me out, I won't make any attempt to stop you.'

When she said nothing, merely waited, he asked, 'What do you know about the way Grant Filey was set up?'

'Only that it began as a joint venture, with each of the partners finding half the capital.'

'So when Conrad Filey left the company, half of it should have been his?'

'Well, yes, I suppose so.'

'After Conrad and my mother were killed, I discovered there was no money. The house was mortgaged up to the hilt and there was nothing left but a pile of debts. I made enquiries and found he'd left Grant Filey without a penny. The whole thing was complicated, but what it added up to was that somehow your father had managed to rob and cheat Conrad out of his share.'

White-faced, Bel said, 'No, that isn't true. Apart from the fact that the company has been struggling financially ever since he left, Dad would never have done a thing like that, believe me.'

'I do believe you. Now. At the time I was furious, and that's when I decided on a take-over. To that end, I approached Mortimer Harmen. When I asked him about the company's financial situation the figures he came up with surprised me. They seemed to indicate that a good half of Grant Filey's assets were gone, yet I knew Conrad hadn't benefited.

'Suspecting that your father had salted the money away, I hired a top private investigator, a man who specialises in uncovering fraudulent behaviour and who is prepared to use unorthodox methods. He gave me his report on Wednesday evening—a report that put a whole new perspective on things.

'My stepfather, it seems, had become an inveterate gambler. Your father discovered what was going on and told him he was being a fool, and that, according to his secretary, who turned out to be a mine of information, was what caused the frequent rows between the two men. Apparently the crunch came when your father discovered a huge discrepancy in the books. He charged Conrad with having taken the money.

'Conrad admitted to having "borrowed" some fifty thousand pounds to pay off a pressing debt, but denied the rest. Your father didn't believe him, and threatened that if he didn't leave the firm the police would be brought in.

'When my investigator managed to examine the accounts he uncovered something strange. The fifty thousand was easy to trace, but a much cleverer, more sophisticated method had been used to systematically cook the books—and it had gone on *after* Conrad had left the company.

'Everything pointed to it having been done by a trained accountant, which convinced me your father was in the clear. I didn't want to show my hand, so I suggested to Hargreaves at the bank that it might be a good idea for him to take a look at the company's books. Your father's response to his request, and also to meeting Conrad's son, only went to prove his complete innocence.

'That left Harmen. As company secretary he was the

obvious suspect... I guessed he was rattled, and might make a run for it, so while you were taking off your wedding dress I told your father briefly what I've just told you, and left him to take whatever action he decided was necessary. I understand that after we'd gone he intended to inform the police.'

'You told Dad *everything*?' Bel demanded hoarsely.

'Not everything. I omitted the part about your stepmother's shares.'

Feeling as though a giant fist was squeezing her heart, she asked, 'Does he know why you married me?'

'Oh, yes, he knows.'

Bel closed her eyes. That was the one thing she'd been hoping to keep from him. Despite all her efforts bitter tears squeezed themselves from beneath her lids and trickled down her cheeks.

'Don't cry, my love.'

The empty endearment was her undoing. Covering her face with her hands, she began to sob.

When Andrew tried to draw her into his arms she pulled away, crying, 'How *could* you be so cruel? You knew before the wedding that Dad wasn't to blame. Why did you go ahead with it?'

'Because I *wanted* to marry you. When I was first planning it, I gathered all the information I could about you. You seemed to be the kind of woman I could like, and from the description I'd been given I guessed that marrying you would be no hardship.

'Then Bentinck showed me some photographs of you and your face haunted me. I knew that even if your father was as guilty as hell I still wanted you. And when I met you I was utterly bowled over, like some callow schoolboy. I thought you were the most enchanting creature I'd ever set eyes on.

'Do you believe in love at first sight? Your father does. I told him how I felt about you and he said, "I felt the same way about her mother."'

When Bel merely stared at him, heartbeat and breathing suspended, Andrew put his hand against her wet cheek and said quietly, 'Please stay. If we try, we can make our marriage work. I know you still think about Bentinck, but in time you'll be able to forget him and—'

But Bel was shaking her head.

She saw Andrew grow pale beneath his tan. 'I suppose I deserve to lose you after all I've done. But, Bel, if your feelings ever change—'

'They won't.' She interrupted him in her turn, and at his look of anguish put her hand over his and turned her mouth into his palm. In a muffled voice she went on, 'I don't still think about Roderick. I know now that all I ever felt for him was liking and affection...'

Andrew stared at her with dawning hope, but not willing to let him off the hook too easily, she added, 'But that doesn't mean I'm prepared to stay with you.'

He reached to open the bedside cabinet and took out a small carefully wrapped package and handed it to her. 'Whether you decide to stay or not, I have a wedding present for you.'

Hands unsteady, she opened the package and caught her breath. The papers relating to the acquisition of Ellen's shares now bore Bel's name, and they were wrapped around a Jesse Harland porcelain figurine of a young girl in jeans, the head tilted slightly, the gaze shy but steady.

Bel lifted eyes brimming with tears to Andrew's face. 'Thank you...I have nothing to give you...' a single bright tear slid down her cheek '...except my love. And I *do* believe in love at first sight. I have to, since it happened to me...'

He muttered something that sounded like, 'Thank God,' and his arms closed round her in an embrace that threatened to bruise her ribs.

'Will you stay?' His voice was hoarse.

She pretended to consider. 'I might, on one condition.'

'Name it.'

'That on the way back to London we make love on the plane. I've always wanted to join the Mile-High Club.'

His little choke of laughter held relief. 'I'm sure that can be arranged.'

Nestling against him, she said seriously, 'I'll let you into a secret. Even if it can't, I don't think I could leave you if I tried.'

His face alight with happiness, he urged, 'Don't try. Stay with me until we're both old and grey and till death us do part... But until then we've a lot of living to do. How shall we start our first full day of married life?'

'What about bacon and eggs for breakfast?'

He kissed the tip of her small straight nose. 'Before or after?'

'Oh, *after*, I think. But first perhaps you'd better put this somewhere safe.' She handed him the figurine.

When he'd put it on the cabinet, he turned and took her in his arms, and with kisses and caresses that held an added dimension of tenderness drew her down into the wild, sweet vortex of passion.

Now, at last, she knew not just how it felt to be made love to, but how it felt to be *loved*.

And it was a wonderful feeling!

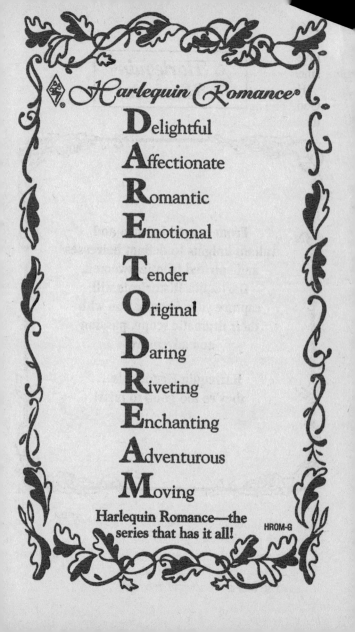

Harlequin Romance®

Delightful

Affectionate

Romantic

Emotional

Tender

Original

Daring

Riveting

Enchanting

Adventurous

Moving

Harlequin Romance—the
series that has it all!

HROM-G

Harlequin® Historical

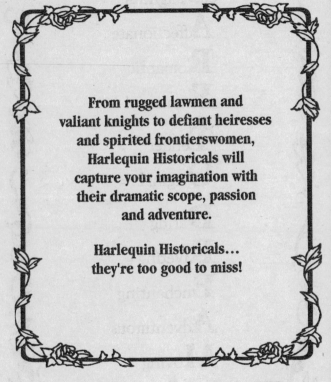

From rugged lawmen and
valiant knights to defiant heiresses
and spirited frontierswomen,
Harlequin Historicals will
capture your imagination with
their dramatic scope, passion
and adventure.

Harlequin Historicals...
they're too good to miss!

HARLEQUIN®
AMERICAN ROMANCE®

LOOK FOR OUR FOUR FABULOUS MEN!

Each month some of today's bestselling authors bring
four new fabulous men to Harlequin American Romance.
Whether they're rebel ranchers, millionaire power brokers
or sexy single dads, they're all gallant princes—and
they're all ready to sweep you into lighthearted fantasies
and contemporary fairy tales where anything is possible
and where all your dreams come true!

You don't even have to make a wish…
Harlequin American Romance will grant your every desire!

Look for Harlequin American Romance
wherever Harlequin books are sold!